nickelodeon

BiG NATE

PRANK YOU VERY MUCH

Inspired by the comics and
book series by Lincoln Peirce

Based on the episodes written by
Sarah Allan, Mitch Watson,
Emily Brundige, and Eric Shaw

Andrews McMeel
PUBLISHING®

Andrews McMeel Publishing
a division of Andrews McMeel Universal
1130 Walnut Street, Kansas City, Missouri 64106

www.andrewsmcmeel.com

Book design, layout, and lettering by The Story Division
www.thestorydivision.com

Editor: Lucas Wetzel
Art Director and Cover Design: Spencer Williams
Designer: Niko Dalcin
Production Editor: Dave Shaw
Copy Editor: Amy Strassner
Production Manager: Chuck Harper

Special thanks to:
Jeff Whitman, Jarrin Jacobs, Nathan Schram, and Flora Liang at Nickelodeon
Steffie Davis, Steve Osgoode, and Niko Dalcin at The Story Division
And special thanks to Lincoln Peirce for editorial guidance throughout this project.

22 23 24 25 26 SDB 10 9 8 7 6 5 4 3 2 1

ISBN (paperback): 978-1-5248-7873-3
ISBN (hardcover): 978-1-5248-7941-9

Library of Congress Control Number: 2022941200

Made by:
King Yip (Dongguan) Printing & Packaging Factory Ltd.
Address and location of production:
Daning Administrative District, Humen Town
Dongguan Guangdong, China 523930
1st Printing — 8/15/22

ATTENTION: SCHOOLS AND BUSINESSES
Andrews McMeel books are available at quantity discounts with bulk purchase for educational, business, or sales promotional use. For information, please e-mail the Andrews McMeel Publishing Special Sales Department: specialsales@amuniversal.com.

CONTENTS

How to Pull a Proper Prank.........5
**BASED ON THE SHORT WRITTEN BY SARAH ALLAN
AND MITCH WATSON**

The Pimple...27
BASED ON THE EPISODE WRITTEN BY EMILY BRUNDIGE

Picture Day 115
BASED ON THE SHORT WRITTEN BY EMILY BRUNDIGE

Time Disruptors..........................137
**BASED ON THE EPISODE WRITTEN BY ERIC SHAW
AND MITCH WATSON**

COMPOSITION

NATE
FILES

WIDE RULE

How to Pull
a Proper Prank

HEY GUYS, NATE WRIGHT HERE! PART OF BEING *AWESOME* IS KEEPING THE FANS HAPPY.

AND WHAT DO MY FANS LIKE MOST? *PRANKS!*

PRANK #1

TODAY WE'LL BE LEARNING ABOUT *CLIMATE CHANGE.*

MY MOM SAYS CLIMATE CHANGE IS THE *HOAX* INVENTED TO DISMANTLE CAPITALISM!

UGH!

6

SIGH.
WELL, IT'S REAL. I'LL PROVE IT TO YOU!
"LET'S HIT PAUSE FOR A SECOND..."
WHAT MR. GALVIN DOESN'T KNOW IS THAT I SLIPPED A BURRITO IN HIS POCKET...
...AND HID CHAD IN THE CABINET...
...DRESSED AS A RAT!

CHAD WILL DO *ANYTHING* FOR A BURRITO! SO WHEN HE SMELLS IT ON GALVIN...?
LET'S WATCH!

GRRRRR!
SNIFF!
SNIFF!

!
BURRITO!
AHHHHHH!
ONE OF THE LAB RATS MUST HAVE GOTTEN INTO MY GROWTH SERUM!
SPROING!

AHHHH!!

ARGHHHH!
AHHHH!!
SHLURRRP!

WAHHH!
EEEEK!
SHLURP!

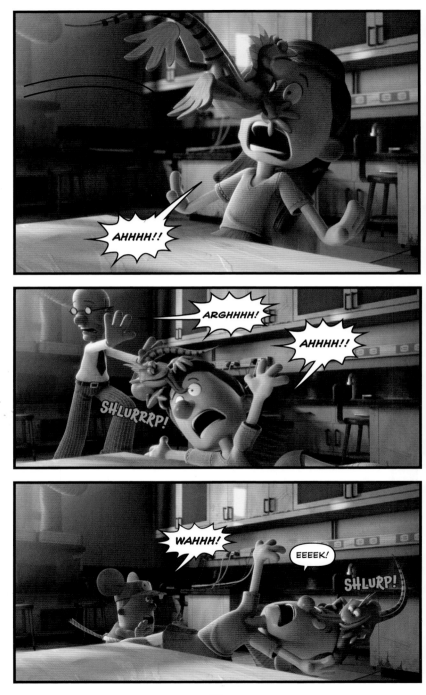

EVER SINCE GINA—MY NEMESIS AND ALL-AROUND KISS-UP—SAW A VLOG ABOUT HOW YOU SHOULD DRINK WATER TO FIGHT ACNE, SHE'S BEEN DEEPLY PASSIONATE ABOUT HYDRATION!
LET'S HAVE SOME FUN, SHALL WE?
PRANK #2
WHICH ONE OF YOU LITTLE TOAST-HEADS CAN TELL ME WHEN THE DECLARATION OF INDEPENDENCE WAS SIGNED?
ANYONE?

ME! ME! *I* KNOW THE ANSWER, MRS. GODFREY!
AUGUST 2ND, 1776!
CORRECT AGAIN, STAR PUPIL!
GROAN!

SWIPE!
KLINK!
GLUG!
GLUG!
GLUG!

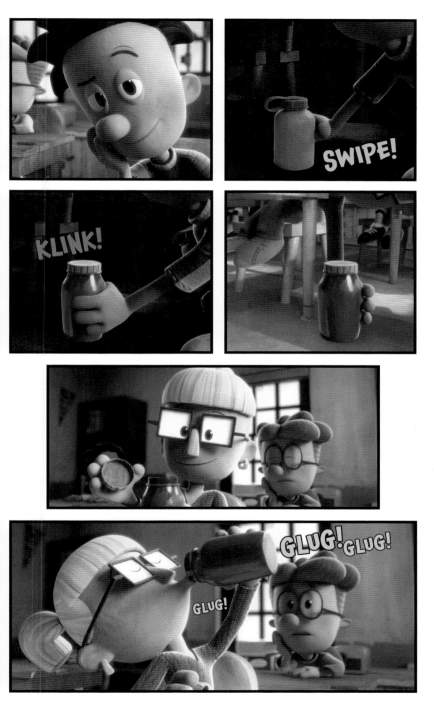

GAG!
RIBBIT!
AHHHHHH! THEY'RE LICKING MY EYEBALLS!
GROOOAAKK

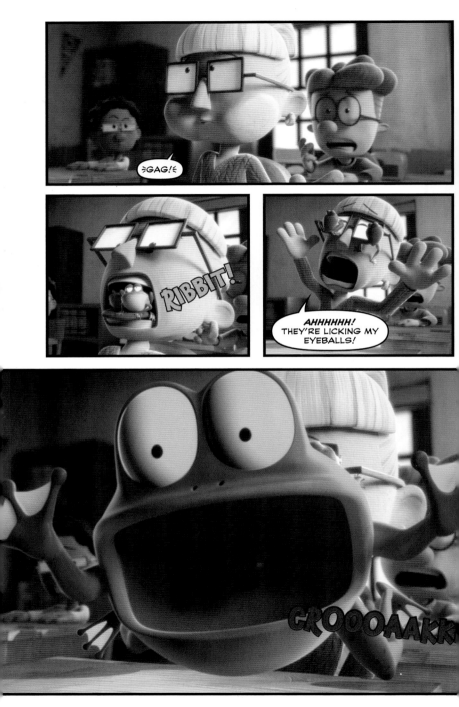

SOME OF MY GLOBAL FANBASE HAS ASKED IF I'VE EVER PRANKED MY FRIENDS? WELL, ***YES!*** IT'S BASICALLY MY SIGNATURE MOVE!
PRANK #3
AHHHHH!
BOINGGG!
CRASHHH!
OOOF!
DING!

PRANK #4
GRUNT!

YOU GUYS WANNA TRY SOMETHING REALLY TOUGH? YOU SHOULD DO ***ATOMIC SIT-UPS!***

LIE BACK, CLOSE YOUR EYES, THEN TRY TO DO A SIT-UP.
YOU'LL SEE. IT'S ***STUPID HARD.***

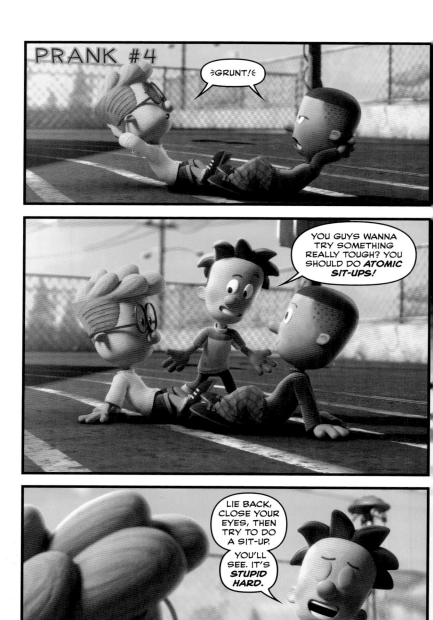

HUH?!
AHAHAHAHAHAHA!
HA
HA
HA
HA
HA
HA
DING!

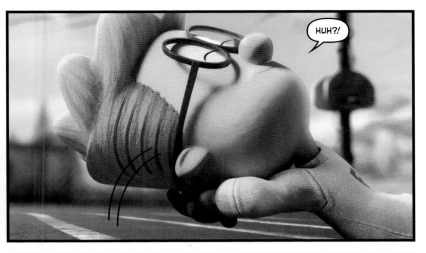

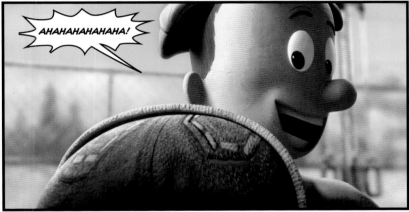

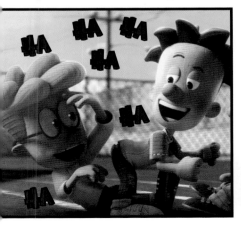

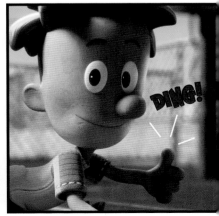

ALWAYS REMEMBER, IF YOU DISH IT OUT, YOU GOTTA BE WILLING TO TAKE IT!
PRANK #5
OH HO!
HEH HEH HEH!
SQUISH!

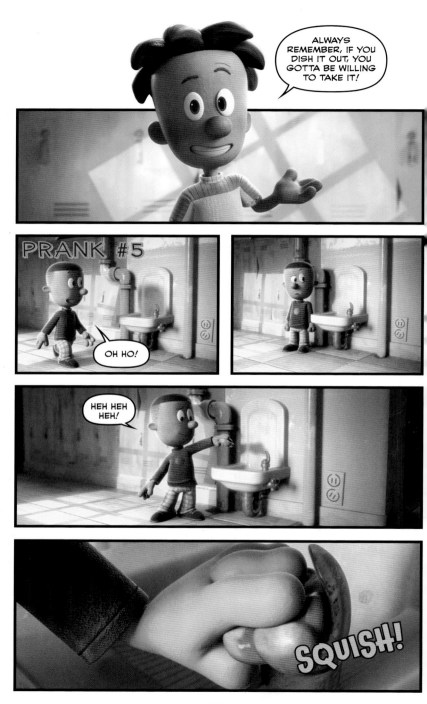

HMM?
BLOOOP!
AHHHHHHH!
POP!
GAME RESPECTS GAME.

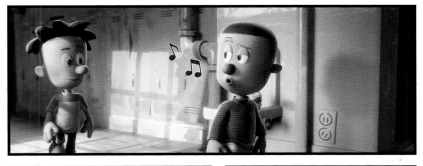

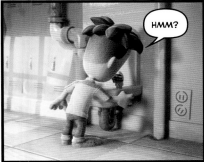

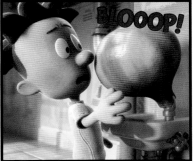

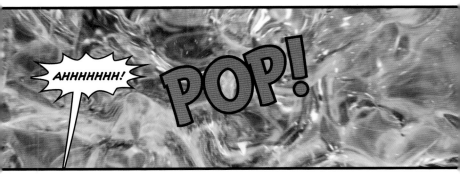

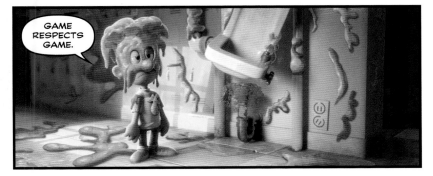

AN OFT FORGOTTEN PRANKING **GOLD MINE** IS THE FAMILY HOME!
PRANK #6
BRUSH BRUSH BRUSH!
PTOO!
HUH?!

AHHHHHH!
HAHAHA!
CLICK!
NATE!!!
I THINK IT'S AN *IMPROVEMENT!*
AHHHHHH!

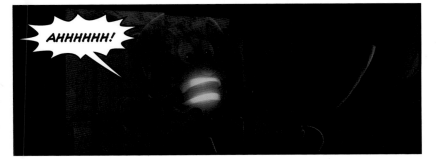

PRANK #7
ZZZZZZ!
OH, HEY SPITSY!
GRRRRRRRR!
GASP!

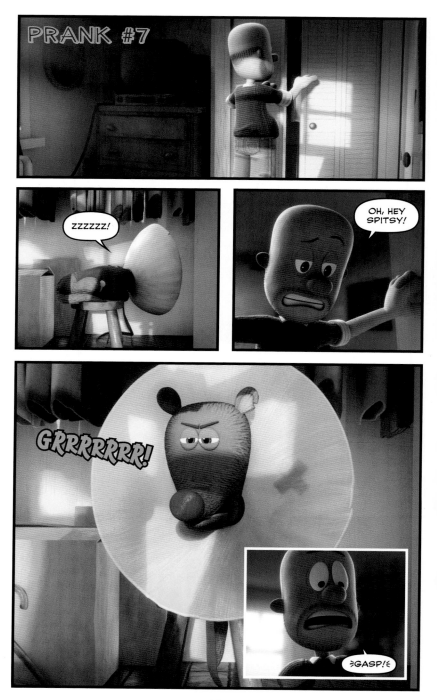

AHHHHHH!

GRR!

CRASH!

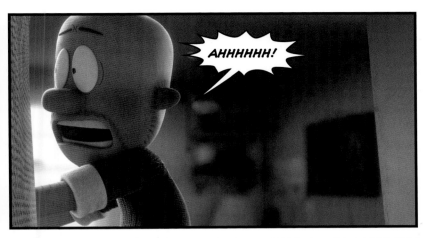

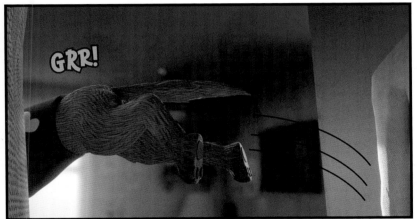

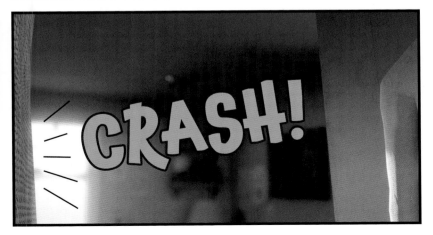

WHEN IT COMES TO PRANKS, YOU JUST GOTTA LET YOUR CREATIVE JUICES FLOW! YOU GOTTA **OWN IT.** BE YOU. **BE AWESOME!**
IS THAT **MY** PHONE?!
UH-OH!
CRASH!

DAD!
OWW, MY ELBOW!
GIVE IT BACK!
OW! DAD, ELLEN HIT ME!
UH, CAN SOMEONE PLEASE HELP ME GET THE NEIGHBOR'S DOG OFF MY BUTT?!
DING!

The Pimple

COMPOSITION
NATE FILES
WIDE RULE

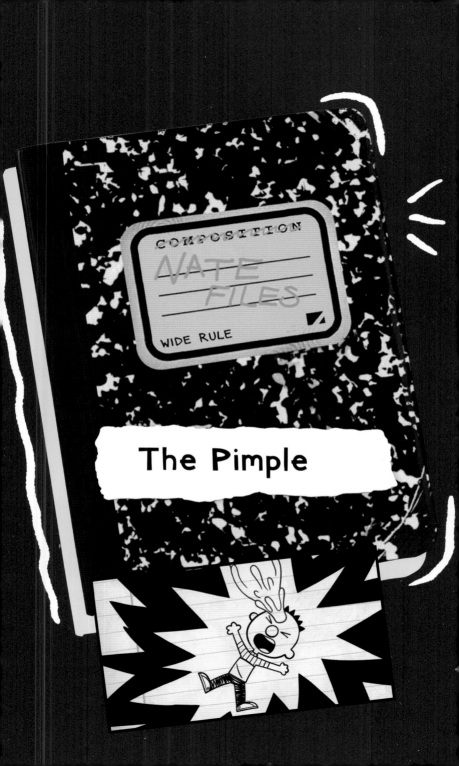

Chapter 1
THIS IS BAD!
ZZZZZ...
CHIP
YAWNNN!
CHIP
AHHHHH!
CHIP
THUD!

YAWN!
HUH?
AAHHHH!

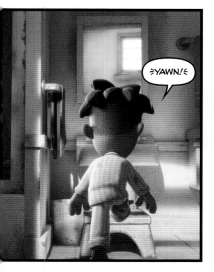

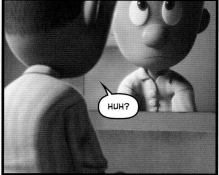

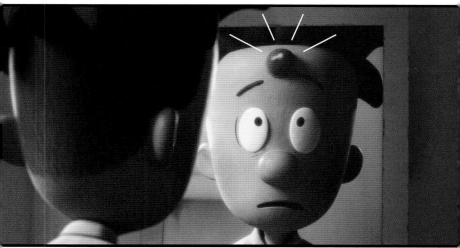

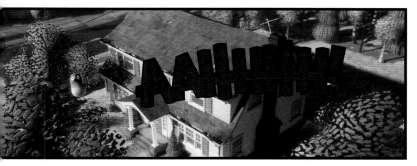

OH, THIS IS BAD! THIS IS LIKE WORLD WAR III WRAPPED UP IN A ZOMBIE APOCALYPSE BAD!
HEY, DORK, GET OUT OF THE BATHROOM! *GASP!* WHA-WH-WH-WHAT?!
OH, MAN! AND YOU CALL ME THE ZIT QUEEN! AHAHAHAHAHA!
SHUT YOUR PIPE, ELLEN!
I HAVE THIS TOTALLY UNDER CONTROL!
WHAT DO I DO?! IF I SHOW UP TO SCHOOL WITH THIS THING, I'M GONNA BE SHAMED!
"MOCKED!
HAHA!
HA
HA HA
HAHA!
"LAUGHED AT!
HAHA!
HA
HA
HAHAHA!
HAHAHA!

"OH, HOW THEY'LL LAUGH!"
EARTH=
HA HA HA
HA HA HA!
HA HA HA
HA HA HA HA!
THERE'S ONLY ONE THING FOR ME TO DO...
SQUEEZE!
WHOA, WHOA, WHOA!
POPPING IT IS ONLY GOING TO MAKE IT A MILLION TIMES WORSE! I SHOULD KNOW, I AM THE ZIT QUEEN!
A MILLION TIMES WORSE? WHAT DID OLD CACKLE PANTS MEAN BY THAT?!

"WILL MY PIMPLE SEEK *REVENGE?*
AHHHH!
ROOAAAR!
"WILL IT BECOME AN *UNSTOPPABLE MEGA PIMPLE BLOB?!*

AHHHH!
ROOAAAR!

"WILL IT MEAN... THE END?!"
NATE
SOB!
WAHHHHH! HE WAS SO YOUNG!

YOU KNOW WHAT? I THINK I BETTER TRUST ELLEN ON THIS ONE. AFTER ALL, SHE IS THE ZIT QUEEN.

AND HEY... MAYBE NO ONE WILL NOTICE!
ZIP!

LATER, AT SCHOOL.
...AND THAT'S WHY A HOT DOG IS DEFINITELY A SANDWICH!
NATE, WHY ARE YOU SNEAKING...
PIMPLE!
SLINK!
I CAN ALWAYS DEPEND ON YOU, DEE DEE.
THAT IS ONE HONKIN' ZIT!
CAN I TOUCH IT?
WHAT? NO!
DOES IT HURT?
I MEAN, NOT REALLY...
DO YOU FEEL DIFFERENT? LIKE, MORE MATURE?

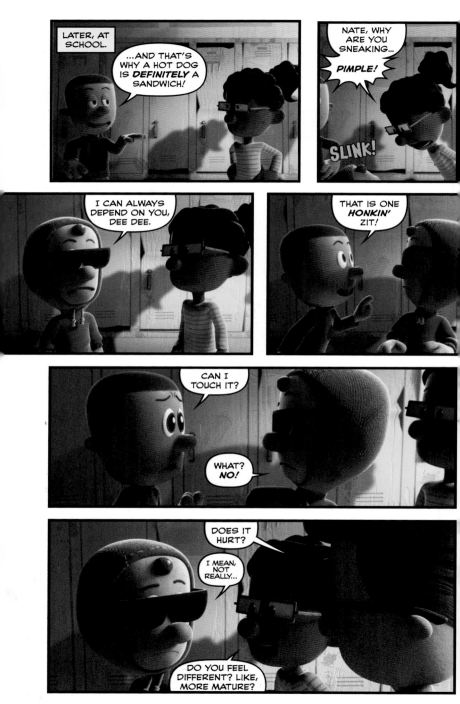

ONE STEP CLOSER TO MANHOOD? SPILL IT!
NO! GEEZ, YOU GUYS, C'MON.
AM I THE FIRST ONE IN OUR GROUP TO GET A PIMPLE?
GUESS SO!
OH, HEY, NATE! COOL PROSTHETIC PIMPLE!
CHAD, IT'S REAL.

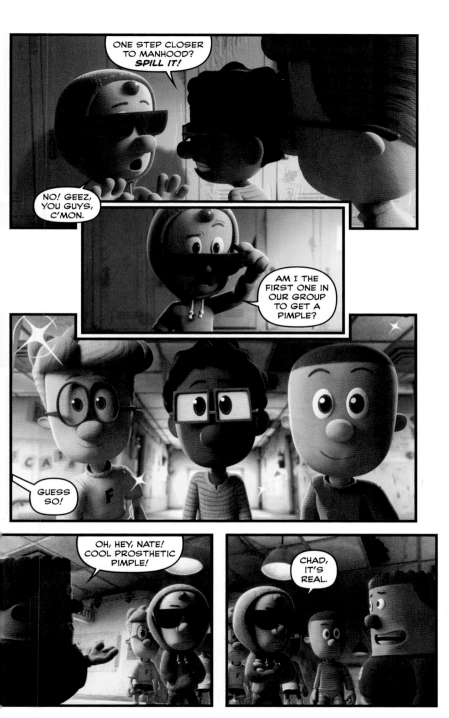

OH, NO KIDDING! YOU SHOULD GET A GOOD PHOTO OF THAT.
"I ALWAYS CATALOG THE GOOD ONES."
AH, MEMORIES. SIGH!
CAN WE PLEASE MOVE ON?
I GOT BIGGER PROBLEMS THAN PIMPLES. I THINK I REALLY FLUBBED MY SCIENCE TEST!

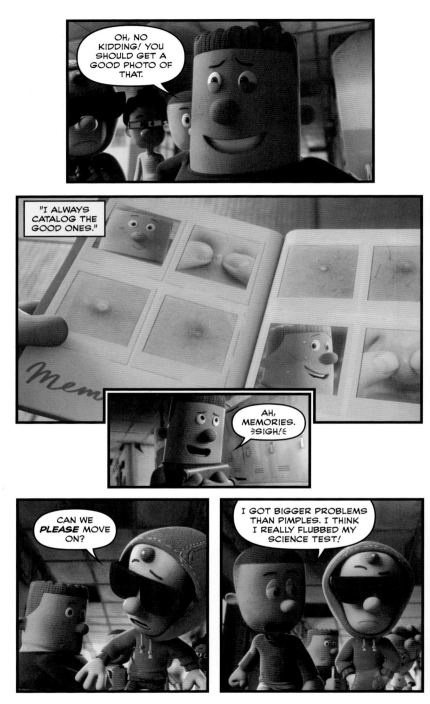

WHAT HAPPENED? I THOUGHT YOU STUDIED!
WELL, YEAH, I WAS GOING TO STUDY, BUT I HAD TO HELP UNCLE PEDRO TRAIN FERRETS FOR HIS RODENT CIRCUS!
DIDN'T HAVE THE HEART TO TELL HIM FERRETS AREN'T RODENTS.
YOU KNOW WHO IS A RODENT? MY DRAMA TEACHER, DR. LAGAZE!
HE KEEPS CASTING ME IN SMALLER AND SMALLER ROLES. THIS SEMESTER, I'M PLAYING THE ROLE OF THE SEAWEED IN "DEATH OF A SAILORMAN."
THE *SEAWEED!* TALK ABOUT TALENT *WASTED!*

JUST LEMME TOUCH IT!

OOOOOH! PLEASE, NATE...
I'VE BEEN FASCINATED WITH PIMPLES SINCE I WAS A BABY!
SHOVE!

YOU'RE GONNA DRAW MORE ATTENTION TO IT!
MIGHTY FINE PIMPLE THERE, NATE!

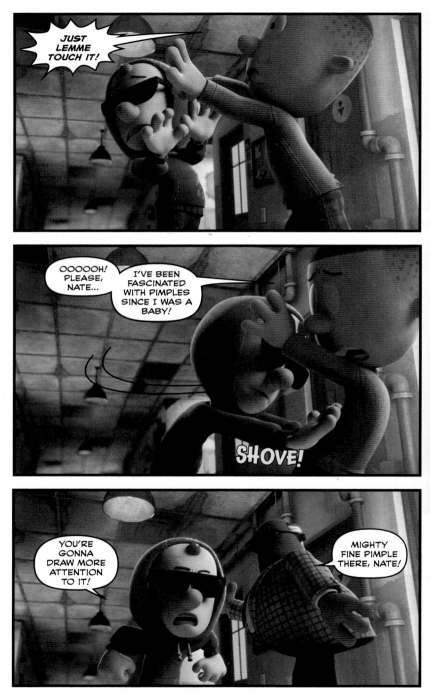

AWWWW! NATE-NATE'S GOT A PIMPIE! HAHAHA!
AH! AHHH!

AHHHH!!!!

GOTCHA!
DOINK!

BOING!
BOING!
BOING!
I FEEL PERSONALLY VIOLATED.

LATER, IN REHEARSAL.
AAAND, ACTION!
LOOK AT ME, FATHER! YOUR BOY IS A SAILORMAN, THIGHS SADDLED IN BRINE.
I MARRIED AN OYSTER ALL SO ONE DAY YOU'D SAY... "I LOVE YOU, MY SAILOR BOY."
BRAVO, RANDALL! BRAVO!
NOW THAT IS WHAT I CALL–
–OOF!
THUMP!
ARGH!
WHAM!

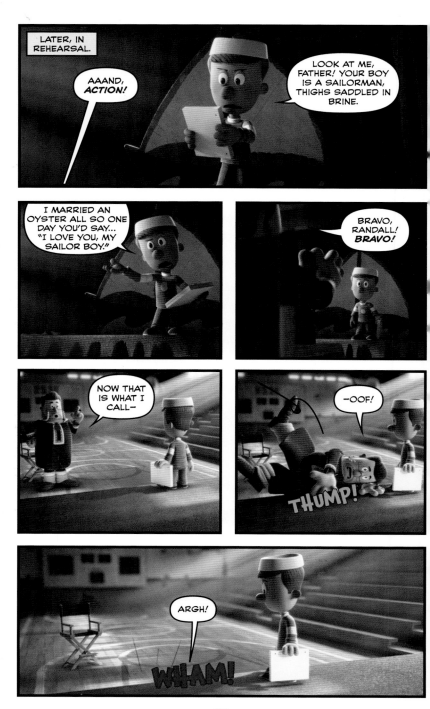

FLIP!
—ACTING!
BUT HE WASN'T SHOWING ANY EMOTION!
EMOTIONS ARE FOR BABIES AND POETS. WE ARE ACTORS!
ALL WE HAVE TO REMEMBER IS OUR DRAMATIC PRODUCE.
OBSERVE.

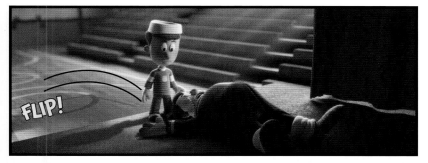

THE ONION!
FSSSSP!
SOB!
OH, TRAGEDY! MY DOG HAS RUN AWAY!
THE BANANA!
OH, JOY! MY DOG HAS RETURNED!

THE TOMATO!

OH, AGONY!
SPLAT!

HE'S JUST BITTEN MY LEG.

MMM, THE FLAVOR!

AS LIFE IMITATES ART, SO TOO SHALL I HAVE TOMATO SOUP FOR LUNCH!
HI! MR. LAGAZE?

PLEASE! I HAVE A ***DOCTORATE*** IN ***DRAMATIC PRODUCE!***
SORRY. ***DOCTOR...*** LAGAZE.
I HAD SOME QUESTIONS ABOUT MY CHARACTER, THE SEAWEED?
GO ON. I'M ***SORT OF*** LISTENING.
WHAT'S HER BACKSTORY?
IS SHE AWARE OF OCEAN ACIDIFICATION AND THE HAVOC IT'S PLAYING ON CORAL REEFS?
AND HOW DOES SHE ***FEEL*** ABOUT THE SAILORMAN?

YOU'RE A SEAWEED, DEE DEE. YOU'RE SLIMY AND GREEN AND NOBODY LIKES YOU.
OH, AND YOU GO LIKE THIS...
OOOLAA GOOLA GOOLA!
GROAN!

LUNCHTIME.
I'M NOT REALLY SURE WHAT I'M EATING...BUT I THINK MAYBE IT'S A...BEAN?
IZZIT?
OOP! I SAID "ZIT," DIDN'T I? SORRY, NATE, I DIDN'T MEAN TO CALL ATTENTION TO YOUR GINORMOUS PIMPLE.
THAT'S OKAY, CHAD.
HERE, NATE, TRY SOME BEANS, I INSIST!
UH...NO, NOT "CYST"! I WAS TRYING TO SAY...

...HELP ME OUT, DEE DEE! WHAT WAS I TRYING TO SAY?
BLACKHEAD.
NO!
PUSTULE.
I GIVE UP!
SIGH.
WELL, ACCORDING TO DR. LAGAZE, I HAVE NOTHING TO SAY, SO I DON'T EVEN KNOW WHY YOU ASKED ME.
SIGH.
GUYS, GUYS, GUYS! IT'S A DANG MIRACLE!

I GOT AN "A" ON MY SCIENCE TEST! ALL BECAUSE I TOUCHED YOUR ZIT!
YOU'VE GOT A LUCKY PIMPLE, MAN!
C'MON, TEDDY. THAT'S RIDICULOUS! A PIMPLE CAN'T BE LUCKY!
LET ME TRY. COME ON, LADY LUCK!
BOOP!

SEE? I'M STILL A SEA–
SILENCE! I HAVE AN ANNOUNCEMENT TO MAKE! I'M TAKING A LEAVE OF ABSENCE.
HOLLYWOOD CALLED. I GOT A SMASHING ROLE IN A HIT SCIENCE FICTION MOVIE FRANCHISE!
GROAN!
SPLAT!
I'M SO HAPPY I COULD CRY...
SPRITZ!
...OH, THE PAIN!

FAREWELL, MY FORMER STUDENTS AND **LESS TALENTED** COLLEAGUES! GOOD LUCK WITH THE REST OF YOUR HUMDRUM LIVES.

I'M CATCHING THE GLORY TRAIN TO LEGENDVILLE!

OOF!
THUMP!

I'M FINE. JUST A LITTLE ONION BLINDNESS.

IS IT A MERE COINCIDENCE THAT DEE DEE TOUCHED MY PIMPLE AND NOW HER BLOWHARD DRAMA TEACHER'S GOING AWAY?
I THINK ***NOT!*** SOONER OR LATER, AWESOMENESS ***ALWAYS*** HITS ITS MARK!
GANG, ME AND THIS LUCKY PIMPLE ARE GOING TO CHANGE THE WORLD!

Chapter 2
THE LUCKY PIMPLE!
FRANCIS. MY MAN. TALK TO ME. WHAT DO WE GOT?
AS OF NOW, YOU HAVE ONE PIMPLE BOOKING AT RECESS.
A SIXTH GRADER'S HAMSTER RAN AWAY. SHE'S DESPERATE.
GOOD WORK, FRANCIS.
TEDDY, GREASE ME.
FSSSS!
SQUEAK!

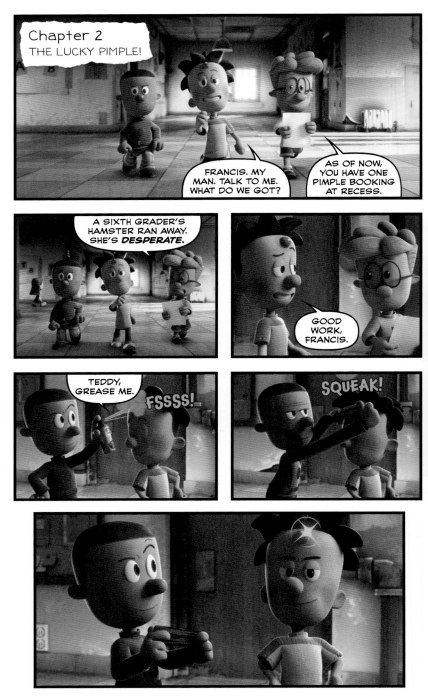

ALL RIGHT, DEE DEE, HOW'S THE DRAMA OUTREACH GOING?
I'M ON IT.
THAT'S WHAT I LIKE TO HEAR.
MM-HMM!
ALL RIGHT, LET'S GO OUT THERE AND SPREAD THE GOOD WORD!

COME ONE, COME ALL! SEE IT FOR YOUR OWN EYES!
BE *AMAZED* BY NATE WRIGHT'S FREAKY-DEAKY *LUCKY PIMPLE!*
A LUCKY PIMPLE?
I WAS ONCE A SKEPTIC LIKE YOU! BUT IT'S THE *REAL DEAL,* MY FRIEND!
AND NOW THAT DR. LAGAZE IS GONE...
OKAY, CLASS, PLEASE TAKE A SEAT.

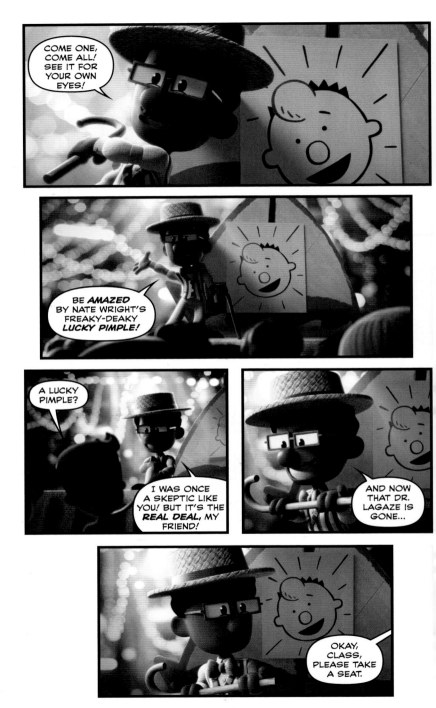

I'M YOUR NEW SUBSTITUTE DRAMA TEACHER.
SHE'S JUST A SUBSTITUTE TEACHER.
LET'S PACK UP THE BACKDROP.
OH. SORRY.
DON'T *EVER* APOLOGIZE FOR BEING OVERLY DRAMATIC!
I'M DONNA!

FWIP!
"D" STANDS FOR DRAMA.
"O" STANDS FOR OBSESSION.

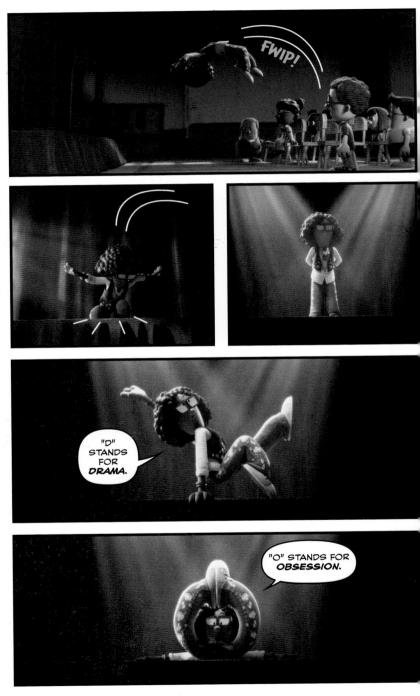

"N" STANDS FOR NURTURE.
THE OTHER "N" ALSO STANDS FOR NURTURE.
THE "A" STANDS FOR...
...ANYWAY, WHAT HAVE YOU GUYS BEEN DOING IN CLASS?

WE'RE SUPPOSED TO BE REHEARSING FOR "DEATH OF A SAILORMAN."
YOU MEAN "SALESMAN"?
NO. IT'S A PLAY OUR OLD DRAMA TEACHER WROTE.
REALLY. CAN I SEE THE SCRIPT?

RRRRRIP!
OHHH!
HUH?
I'M SURE WHATEVER'S HAPPENING IN YOUR OWN LIVES IS MUCH MORE INTERESTING THAN WHAT'S IN THAT SCRIPT.
I LEARNED THAT WHEN I DID MY ONE-WOMAN PLAY, "THE DONNALOGUES," ON BROADWAY.
YOU WERE ON BROADWAY?!

YES, BUT I LEFT IT ALL BEHIND TO PURSUE MY ***REAL*** PASSION.
BEING A ***SUBSTITUTE DRAMA TEACHER!***
NOW, I WANT TO HEAR FROM YOU ALL.
TELL ME SOMETHING THAT HAPPENED YESTERDAY THAT ***MOVED*** YOU.
I CRUSHED A BUG.
AND HOW DID THAT MAKE YOU FEEL?
POWERFUL.
OKAY. THANK YOU...?

RANDY. OR RAD-SAUCE. OR RANDMAN.
OF COURSE... ANYONE ELSE?
MY FORMER DRAMA TEACHER TOLD ME THAT I WAS SLIMY AND GREEN AND THAT **NOBODY LIKED ME.**
AND HOW DID THAT MAKE YOU FEEL?
LIKE THE BUG THAT RANDY—
RAD-SAUCE.
...THAT RAD-SAUCE CRUSHED. I FELT STEPPED ON. IT MADE ME WANT TO **SCREAM!**

SO, WHY DON'T YOU?
AAAAHHHHHHHH
AAAHHHHHHHHHHHH!
BOOM!
BOOM!
CRACK!
CRACK!

THANK YOU... UM?

DEE DEE. THE NAME'S DEE DEE.

CLASS, I WANT YOU ALL TO RECOGNIZE DEE DEE'S *BRAVERY* HERE TODAY.

WOW!

AFTER CLASS.

HUH?

NATE!

NATE! YOU'LL NEVER BELIEVE IT!

THE NEW DRAMA TEACHER'S AMAZING SHE DID THIS DANCE AND HAD A SHOW ON BROADWAY AND SHE THINKS—

WHOA, WHOA. OKAY, DEE DEE, SLOW IT DOWN.

...THINKSSSS... I'MMMMMMMM... BRAAAAAAAAAVE...

YOU KNOW, IN HINDSIGHT, I SHOULD HAVE BEEN MUCH MORE SPECIFIC ABOUT MY INSTRUCTIONS.
NATE WRIGHT!
THAT'S ME.
WHAM!

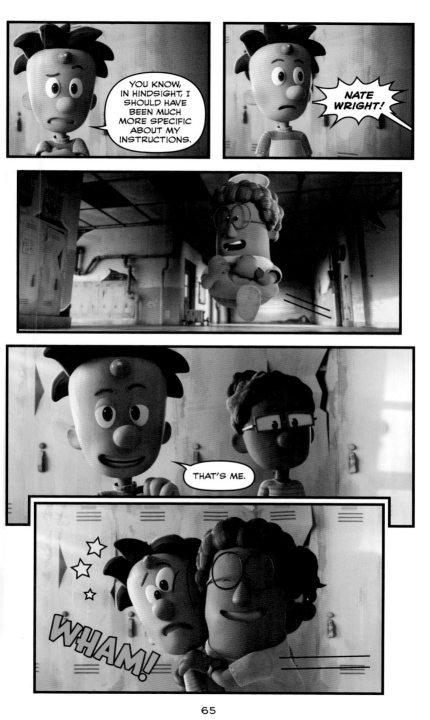

I TOUCHED YOUR PIMPLE THIS MORNING, AND MR. SQUIGGLES CAME BACK TO ME!
DID YOU HEAR THAT?
NATE WRIGHT'S PIMPLE BROUGHT MY HAMSTER BACK!
WELL WHAT DO YOU HAVE TO SAY FOR YOURSELF, NATE WRIGHT?
UH...BLESSED BE THE PIMPLE?

SQUEAK!
BLESSED BE THE PIMPLE!
BLESSED BE NATE WRIGHT!
BLESSED BE THE PIMPLE!
BLESSED BE NATE WRIGHT!

LATER.
STEP UPPETH AND RECEIVE THE PROMISE OF THE PIMPLE!
I TRIED TO CUT MY OWN HAIR AND THIS IS WHAT HAPPENED! NOW I'LL **NEVER** GET A GIRLFRIEND!
THAT'S FOR THE PIMPLE TO DECIDE!
BOOP!

OH, UH, HEY TRENDSETTER! HOT HAIRCUT! WANNA CUT MY HAIR LATER?
!!!
NATE, MY LEG IS BUSTED AND THE CHAMPIONSHIP GAME IS NEXT WEEK!
AH, YES, THE GREAT PIMPLE HAS HEARD YOU!
BOOP!

BY THE POWER OF THE PIMPLE, I SHALL BECOME THE *ULTIMATE* SOCCER PLAYER!
HI-YA!
CRSSSH!
HEADS UP!
FWOOSH!
BLAM!
WHAM!
OOF!
ALL GOOD!

LATER.
GOTTA KEEP THIS PIMPLE FED!
SPLOOSH
RUB!
RUB!
RUB!
SLURP!
GASP!

THE PRINCIPAL'S OFFICE.
NATE, HERE'S THE BOTTOM LINE...
...I GOT A TIP ON SOME MONKEY-POWERED WINDMILLS, AND... WELL...
OO-OO! AH-AH!
SCREECH!
"IT WAS NOT A GOOD INVESTMENT."
FWOOSH!

I'M BROKE! I JUST NEED ONE BIG SCORE TO GET ME BACK ON MY FEET!
LET ME TOUCH YOUR PIMPLE, AND I ***PROMISE*** YOU'LL NEVER HAVE TO GO TO DETENTION FOR THE ***REST*** OF YOUR ***LIFE!***
BOOP!

Chapter 3
RESPECT THE PIMPLE!

THANK YOU, NATE WRIGHT! BECAUSE OF YOU, MY BABY CAN WALK!

COO!

AREN'T BABIES *SUPPOSED* TO WALK AT THIS AGE?

SHOW SOME *RESPECT* FOR THE PIMPLE, HOWARD.

PIMPLE MERCH, PIMPLE MERCH HERE! GET IT BEFORE IT *POPS!*

WHY ISN'T THIS ZIT WORKING?!

YOU CAN'T *FORCE* AWESOMENESS, FELLAS.

MEANWHILE, IN REHEARSAL...
IT WAS THE SUMMER OF MY SIXTH YEAR. I REMEMBER THE SMELL OF HYDRANGEAS.
MY PARENTS WERE HAVING A YARD SALE AND I WAS ASKED TO GET RID OF SOME OF MY STUFFED ANIMALS.
A CHILD SHOULD ***NEVER*** HAVE TO MAKE SUCH A CHOICE!
I TRIED TO TAKE IT BACK, BUT IT WAS TOO LATE. CHARLIE THE PENGUIN WAS GONE! AND I WAS LEFT WITH AN EMPTY SPACE ON MY COMFORTER!

CLAP
CLAP
CLAP
CLAP
CLAP
HONK!
DEE DEE! HANG BACK A MINUTE.
I HAVE SOMETHING FOR YOU.

Uta Hagen
A Challenge for the Actor
WHAT'S THIS?
DEE DEE, I THINK YOU'VE GOT A REAL *GIFT.*
KEEP PRACTICING YOUR CRAFT AND YOU MIGHT JUST FIND THE ACTOR INSIDE THE ACTOR INSIDE THE PERSON INSIDE THE PERSON IN *YOU.*

LATER.
YA KNOW, I CAN EAT ALL THE GREASY FAST FOOD I WANT!
JUST MAKES THE PIMPLE MORE POWERFUL!
GIGGLE!
PTOOO!
NATE! WHAT ARE YOU *DOING?*
I'M JUST SPENDING SOME QUALITY TIME WITH MY FANS.
OH YEAH? WELL ARE THEY HERE FOR YOU, OR FOR YOUR *PIMPLE?!*

≯COUGH!≮ JEALOUS. ≯COUGH!≮ SO PAINFULLY JEALOUS. ≯COUGH!≮ SORRY, I HAD SOMETHING IN MY THROAT. I WAS SAYING YOU'RE JEALOUS.
GRRR!
DON'T LET THAT PIMPLE WRITE A CHECK YOUR BUTT CAN'T CASH!
BOOP!
EWW. REMOVE HER!
NOOO!

YOU CAN'T DO THIS TO ME!
I'M THE ZIT QUEEEEN!
SPLOORSH!
NOM NOM NOM!
SLURP!

THE NEXT DAY.

NOK! NOK!

DEE DEE! WHAT A *LOVELY* SURPRISE!

I FOUND YOUR ADDRESS IN THE SUBSTITUTE TEACHER PAGES.

OH, WHO IS YOUR LITTLE FRIEND, DONNA?

OH, HOW RUDE OF ME! THIS IS KATHLEEN, MY WIFE.
"WIFE"...?
HI, DEE DEE! DON, IS THIS THE ***TALENTED YOUNG ACTRESS*** YOU'VE BEEN TELLING ME ABOUT?

IT CERTAINLY IS.
WELL, UH, SORRY TO JUST SHOW UP AT YOUR HOUSE LIKE THIS, BUT I HAD SOME QUESTIONS ABOUT THIS BOOK.
AS DEDICATED AS I THOUGHT YOU WERE! COME IN, COME IN. I'LL MAKE SOME TEA.

MONDAY AT SCHOOL.

YOU'RE SO WISE, NATE. I CAN'T BELIEVE YOU'RE ONLY IN SIXTH GRADE!

Y'KNOW, YOU'RE NOT THE FIRST SEVENTH-GRADE GIRL TO TELL ME THAT THIS WEEK.

FLY AWAY, LITTLE BIRDIES!
HEY, JENNY!
WOULD YOU LIKE TO TOUCH MY PIMPLE?
GRR! HEY, GIVE ME A TOUCH!
GROSS!!!
EWWW!
NO, JENNY, WAIT!

YOU OKAY UP THERE BUDDY?
NATE!
HOW COULD YOU **DO** THIS TO ME?!
WHAT? WHAT ARE YOU TALKING ABOUT, TEDDY?
BECAUSE OF THE "A" I GOT ON MY SCIENCE TEST, I'M BEING SENT TO A GIFTED SUMMER SCHOOL FOR EXCEPTIONAL CHILDREN!
I'M NOT EXCEPTIONAL **OR** GIFTED!
WELL, NOW YOU'RE JUST STATING THE OBVIOUS...AND NONE OF THAT IS ***MY*** FAULT!

IT'S **ALL** YOUR FAULT! I SHOULD HAVE **NEVER** TOUCHED YOUR PIMPLE. THIS ISN'T MY HAMSTER AT ALL!
MY PARENTS LIED TO ME! IF THEY EVEN **ARE** MY PARENTS!
MY WHOLE LIFE HAS BEEN A LIE!!!
AHHHHH!
YOU! NATE WRIGHT! MY LEG WAS **STILL** BROKEN! NOW I'M GONNA HAVE TO WEAR THIS **HUGE** CAST UNTIL I'M **FORTY!**
AND THEN THEY'RE GONNA HAVE TO STRETCH MY LEG FOR ANOTHER TEN YEARS TO GET IT TO MATCH MY OTHER LEG!
MY SOCCER CAREER IS **OVER!**
GASP!
DO YOU KNOW HOW **HARD** IT IS TO MAINTAIN THIS BAD HAIRCUT? **DO YOU?!**

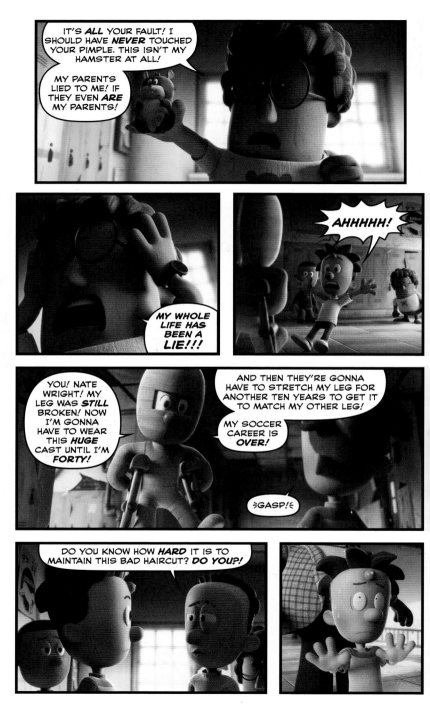

THANKS TO ***YOU*** AND YOUR ***FRAUDULENT*** PIMPLE, MY BIG SCORE DIDN'T PAY OFF AND NOW I GOTTA SKIP TOWN BEFORE SOME ***VERY ANGRY*** MONKEYS TEAR MY FACE OFF!
GRRRR!
DETENTION, EVERY DAY, FOR THE REST OF YOUR LIFE, NATE! DO YOU HEAR ME?!
THE REST OF YOUR LIFE!
PIMPLE, PIMPLE, WHY HAVE YOU FORSAKEN ME?!

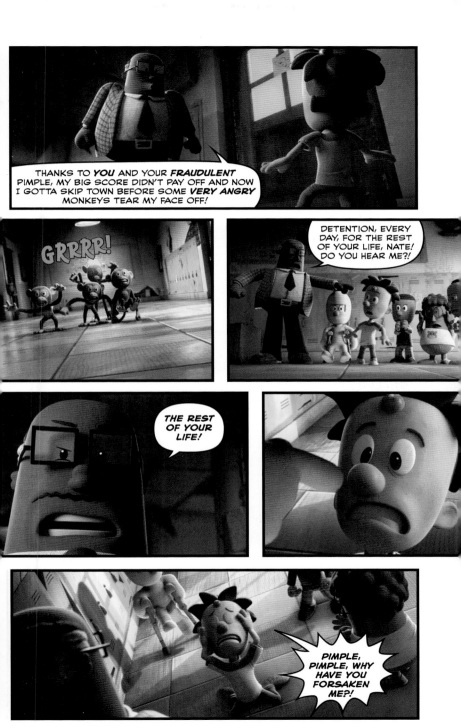

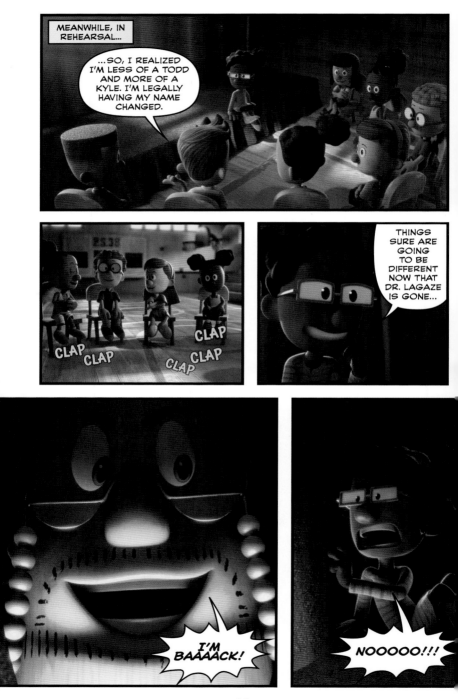

WOOO! YES!

ENOUGH OF THIS CODSWALLOP! TAKE OUT YOUR DRAMATIC PRODUCE!

BOOOO!
AH! OW! OOOH!

AHHH! WHAT AM I GOING TO DO?! WHERE AM I GOING TO GO?!
FWOOP!

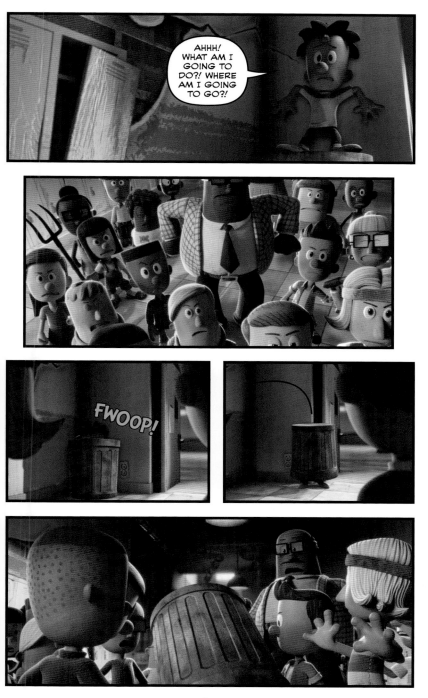

CRRRSH!!

WHAM!

≽PHEW!≼

MY BABY REVERTED BACK TO CRAWLING!

LOOK AT THIS! *PATHETIC.*

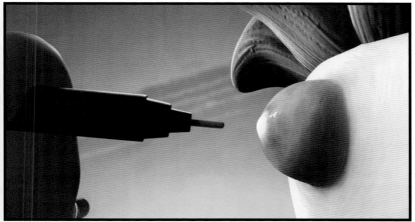

98

SORRY, BROTHER, I CAN'T GO TO THAT LAME SUMMER CAMP FOR BRAINIACS. I'M NOT CUT OUT FOR THAT KIND OF TIME.

HE'S IN HERE, GUYS!

⋛GASP!⋜ ET TU, TEDDY?

⋛GASP!⋜

CRRRSH!!

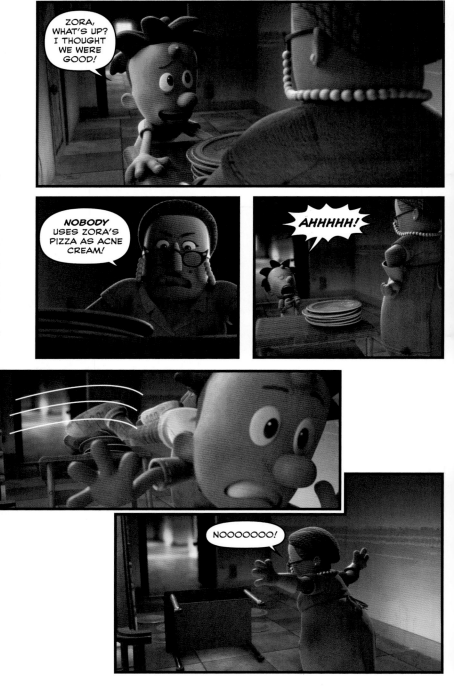

104

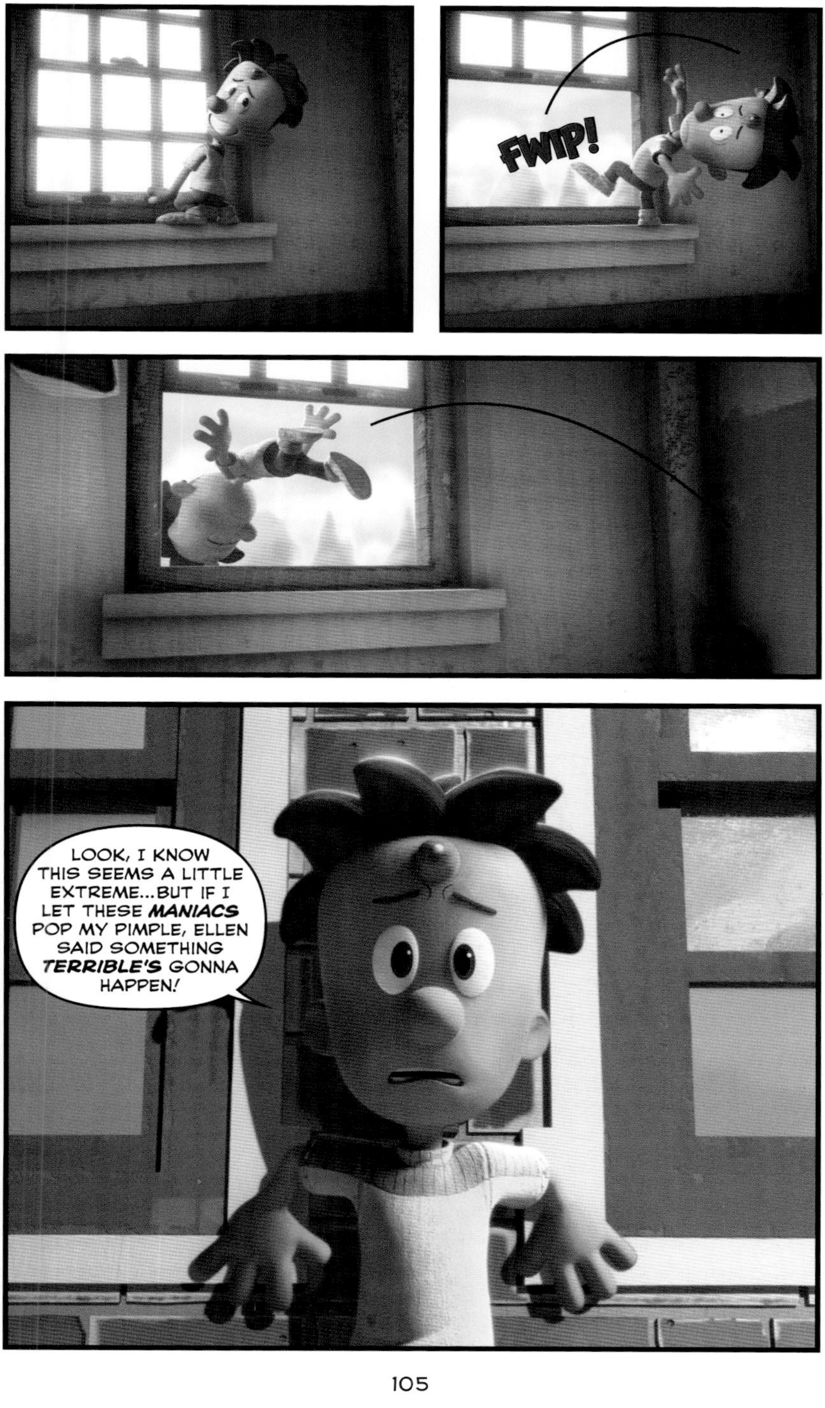
FWIP!
LOOK, I KNOW THIS SEEMS A LITTLE EXTREME...BUT IF I LET THESE ***MANIACS*** POP MY PIMPLE, ELLEN SAID SOMETHING ***TERRIBLE'S*** GONNA HAPPEN!

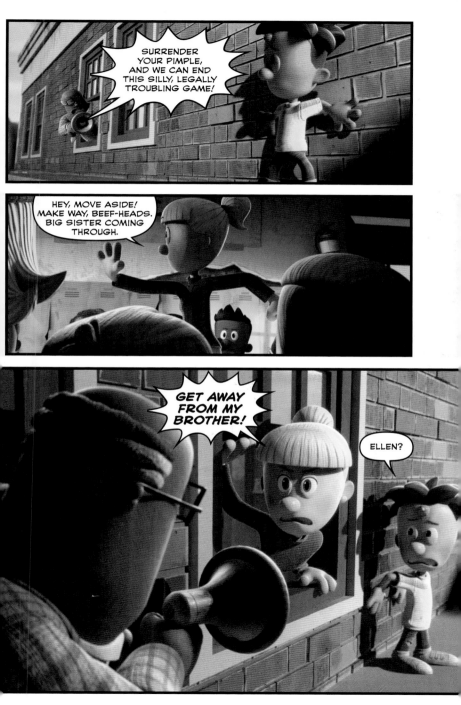

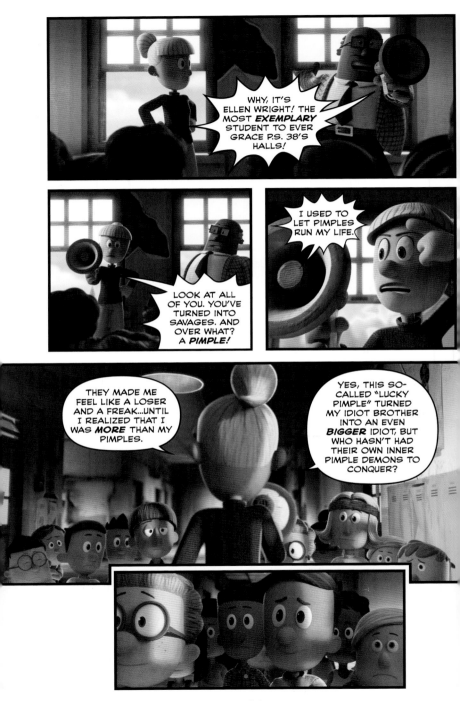

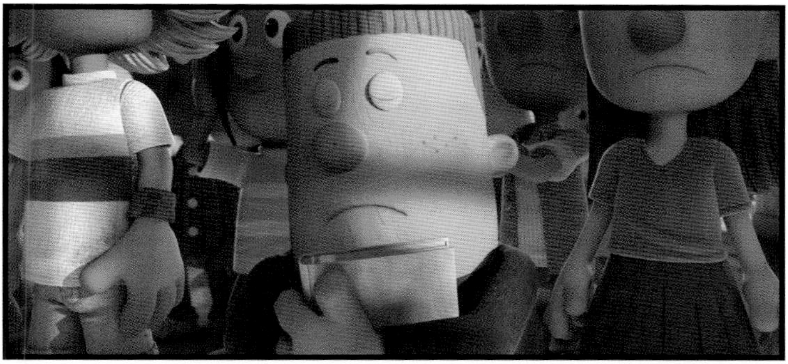

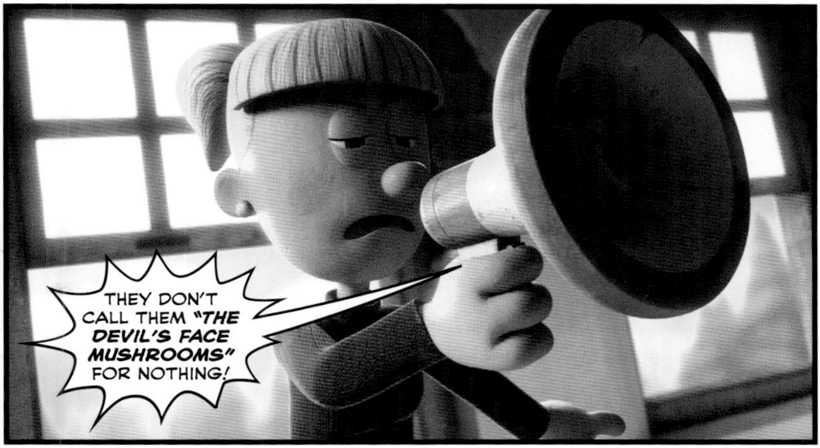
THEY DON'T CALL THEM *"THE DEVIL'S FACE MUSHROOMS"* FOR NOTHING!

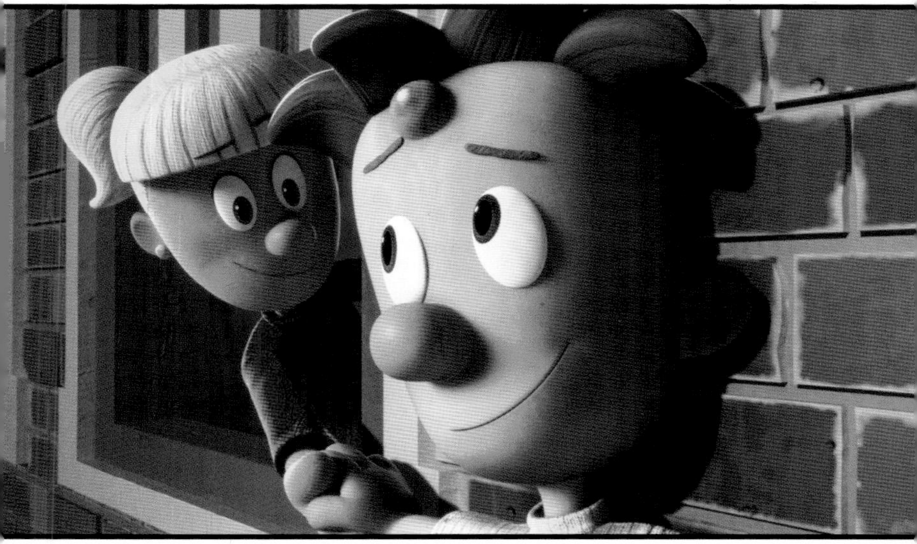

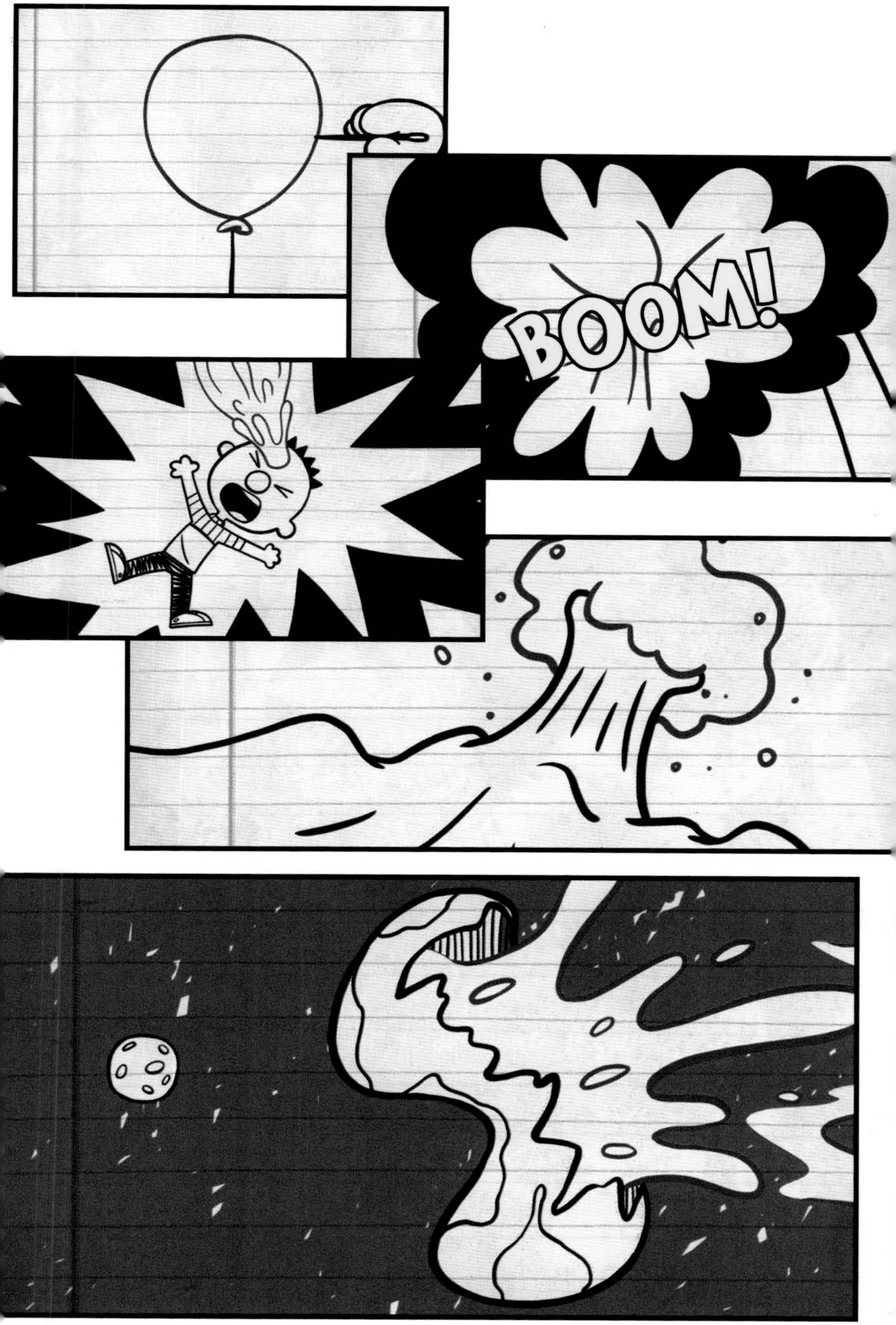
BOOM!

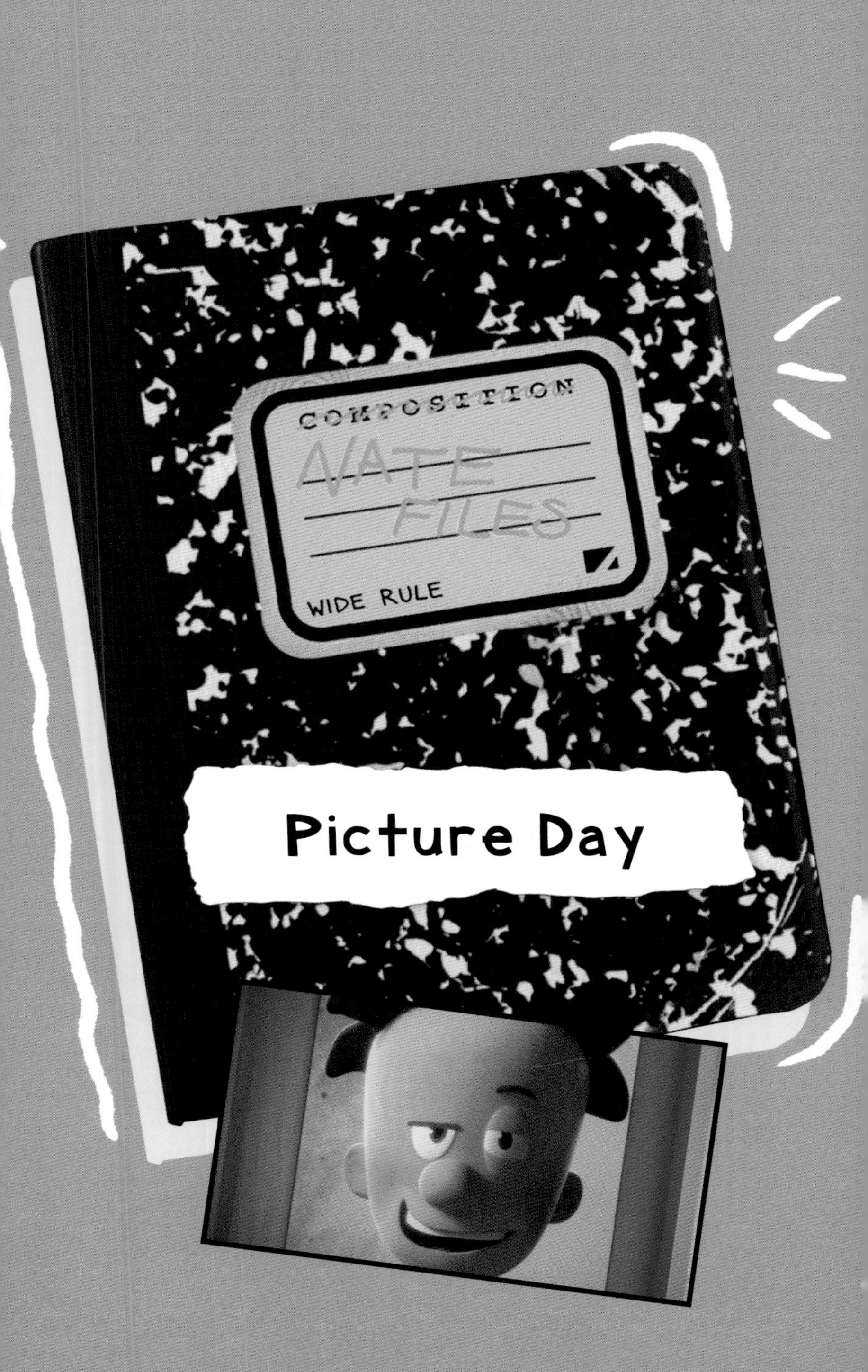
COMPOSITION
NATE FILES
WIDE RULE
Picture Day

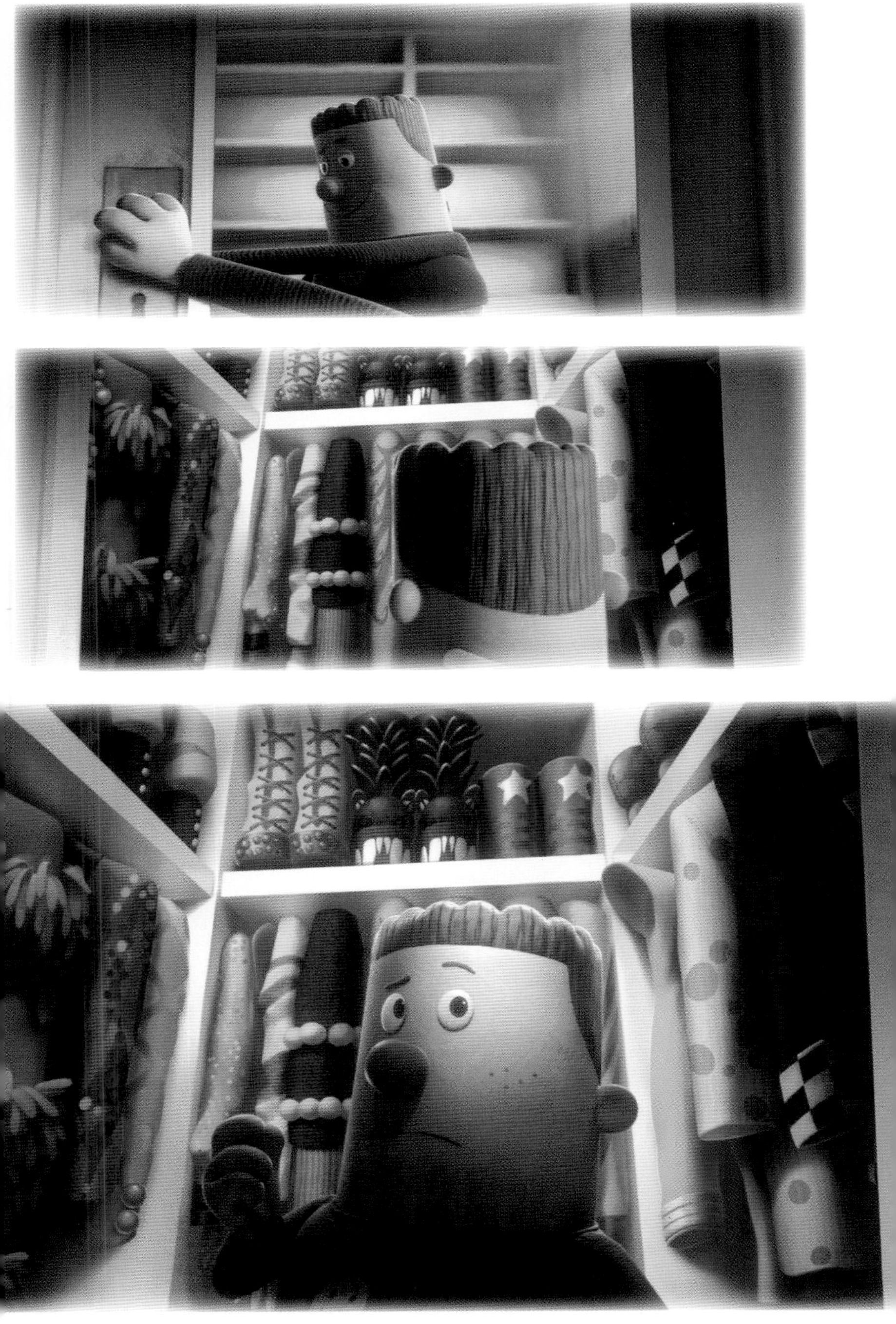

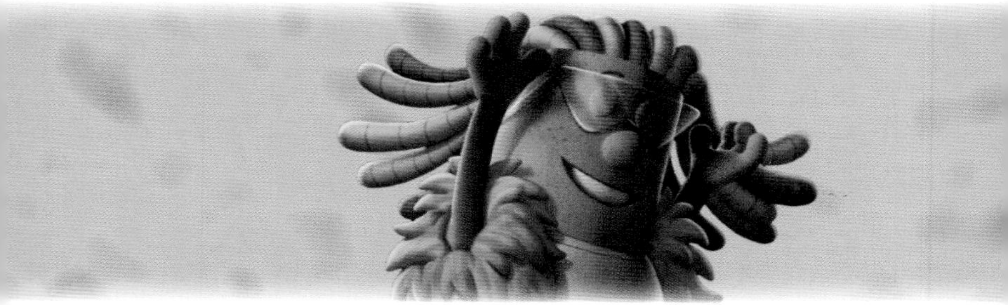

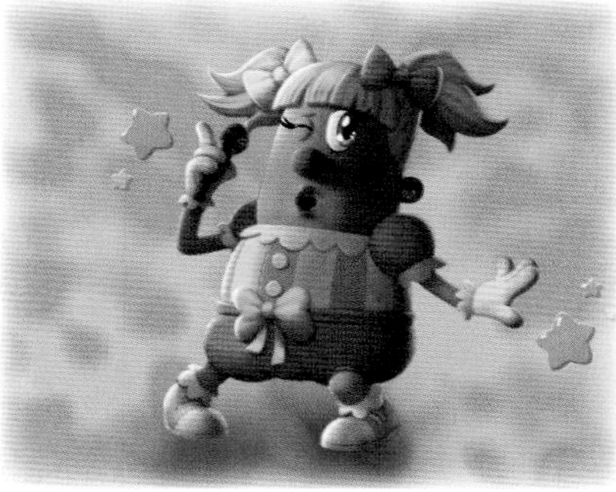

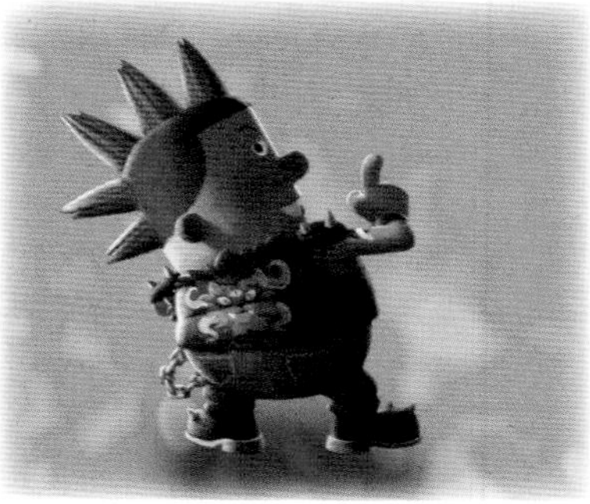

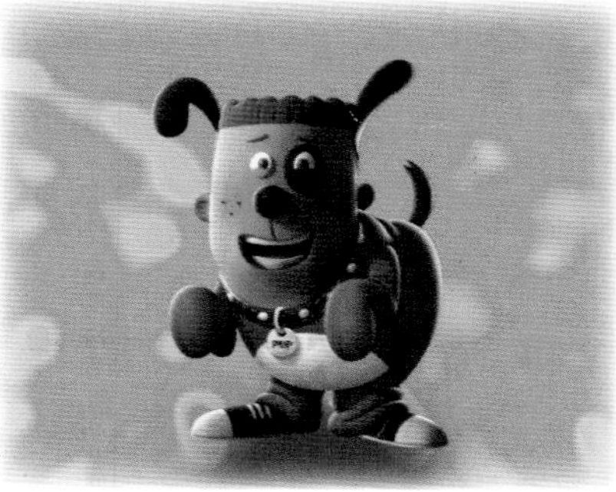

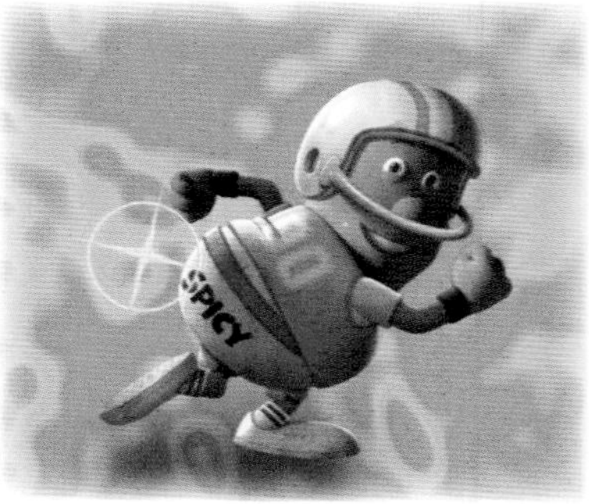
SPICY

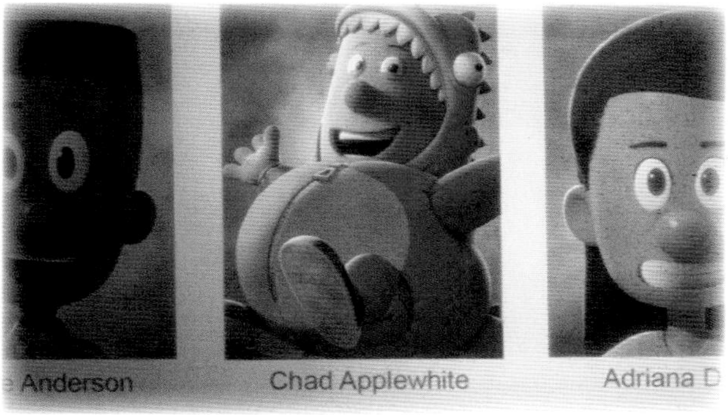
Anderson
Chad Applewhite
Adriana D

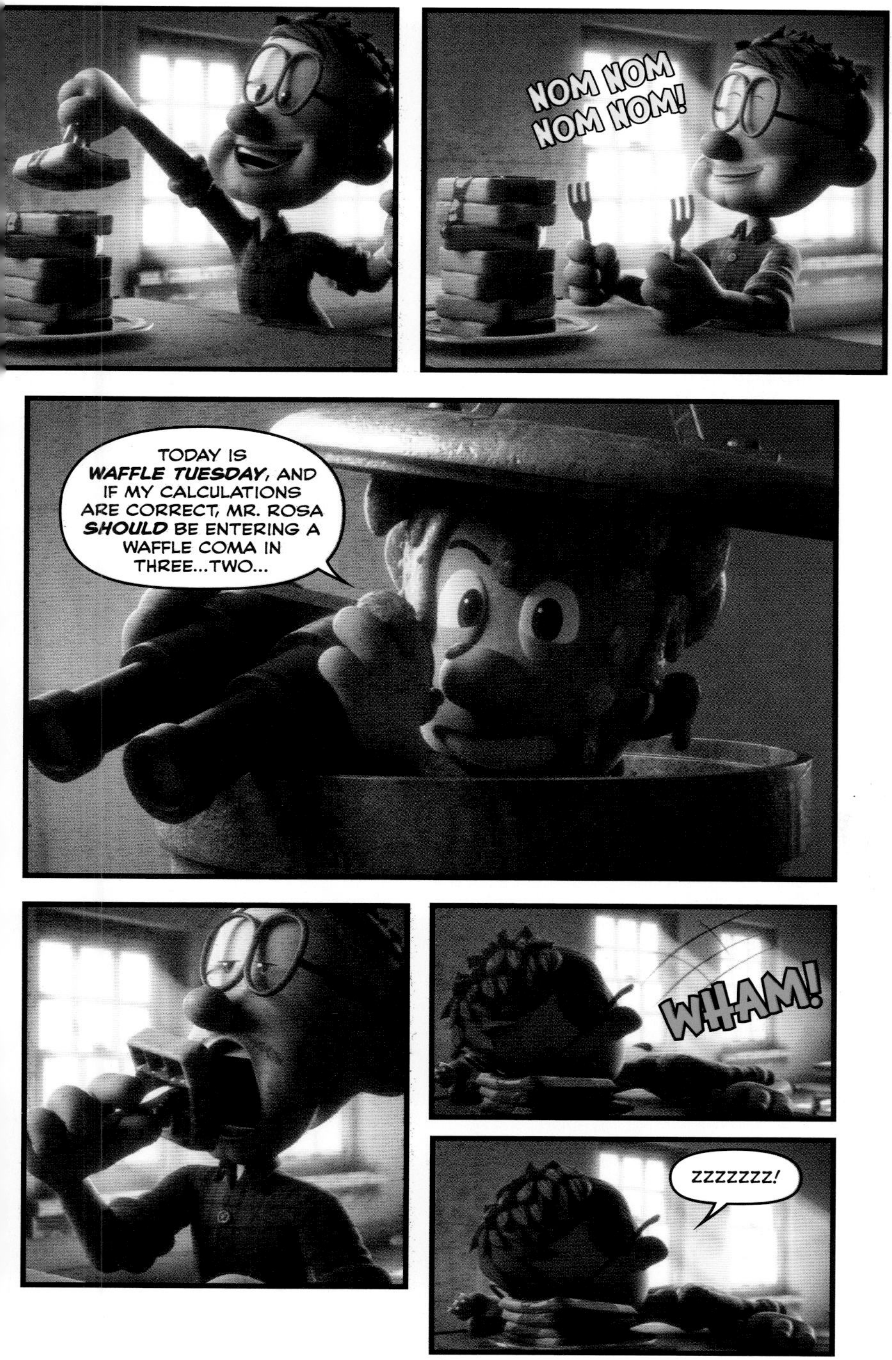

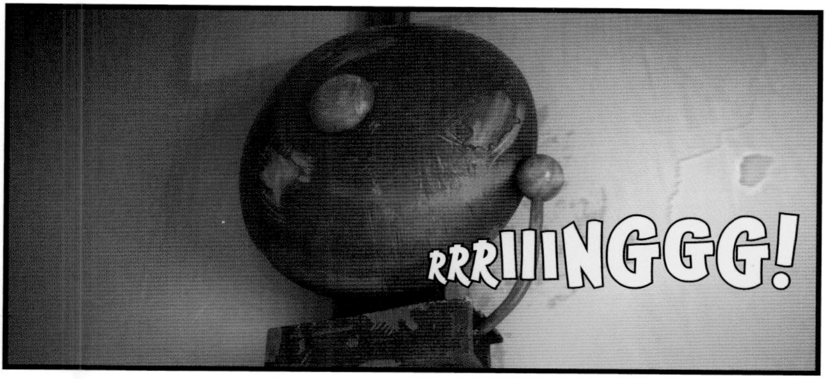
RRRIIINGGG!

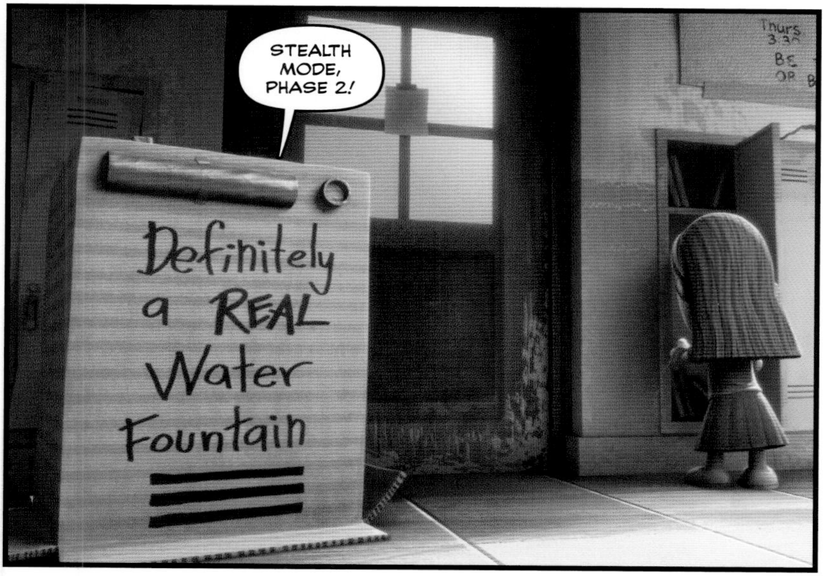
STEALTH MODE, PHASE 2!
Definitely a REAL Water Fountain

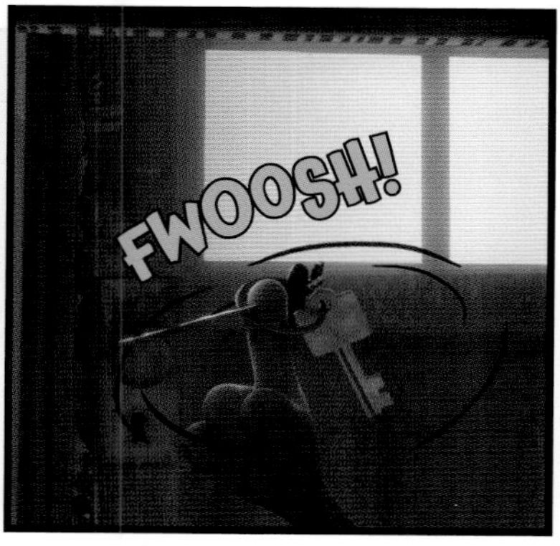
FWOOSH!

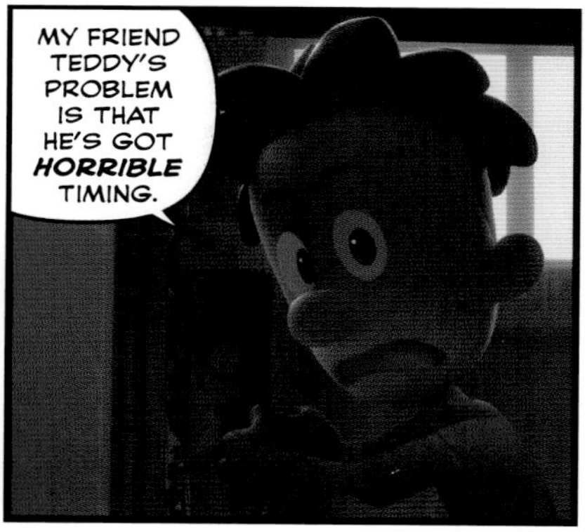
MY FRIEND TEDDY'S PROBLEM IS THAT HE'S GOT ***HORRIBLE*** TIMING.

Ellie Mills   Teddy Ortiz   Nichole Phillips

126

127

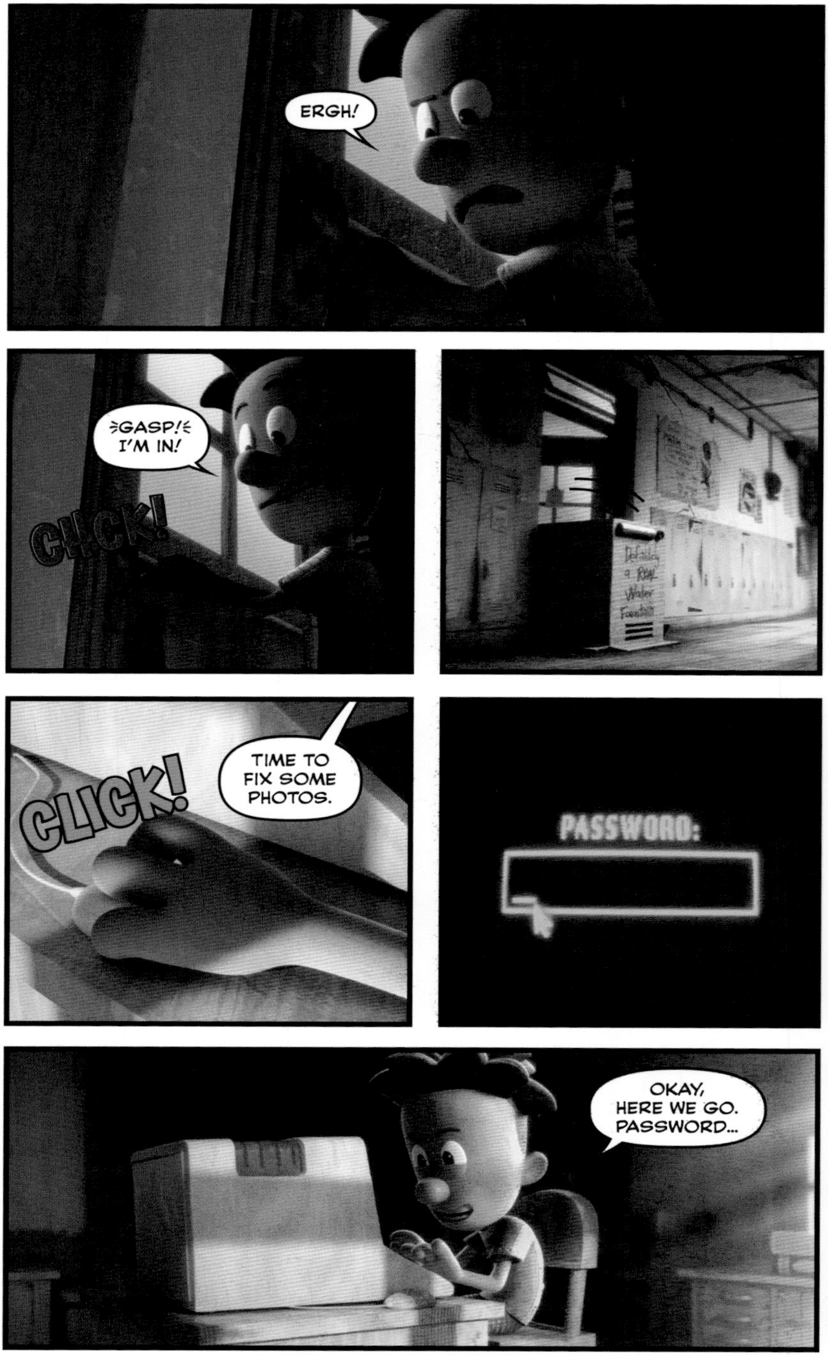
ERGH!
GASP! I'M IN!
CLICK!
Definitely a REAL Water Fountain
TIME TO FIX SOME PHOTOS.
CLICK!
PASSWORD:
OKAY, HERE WE GO. PASSWORD...

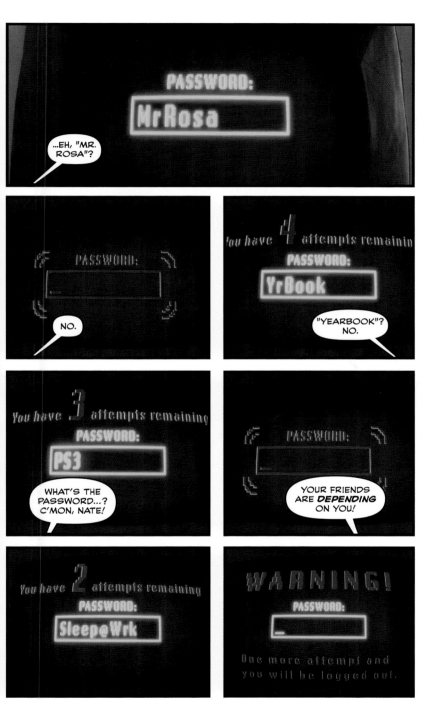

129

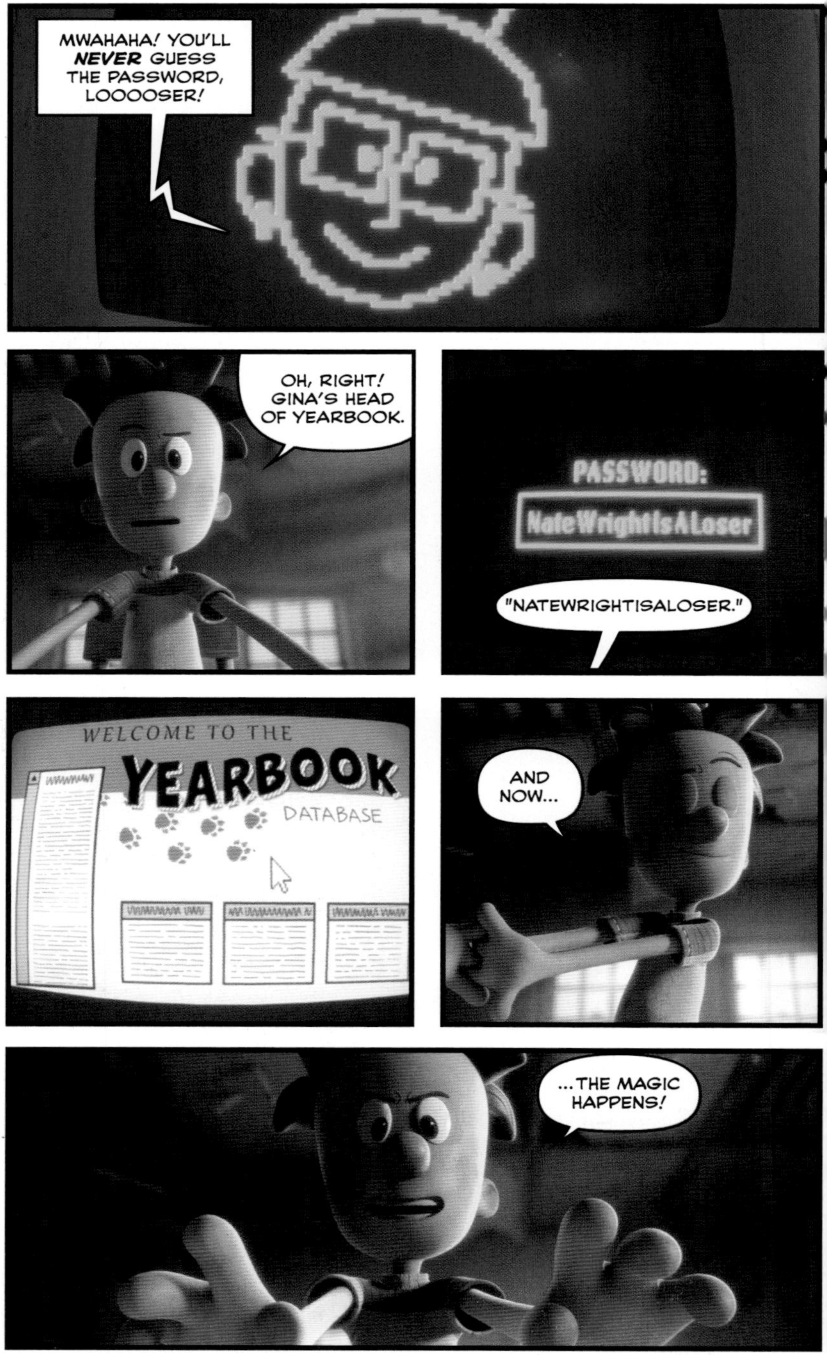
MWAHAHA! YOU'LL **NEVER** GUESS THE PASSWORD, LOOOOSER!
OH, RIGHT! GINA'S HEAD OF YEARBOOK.
PASSWORD:
NateWrightIsALoser
"NATEWRIGHTISALOSER."
WELCOME TO THE
YEARBOOK
DATABASE
AND NOW...
...THE MAGIC HAPPENS!

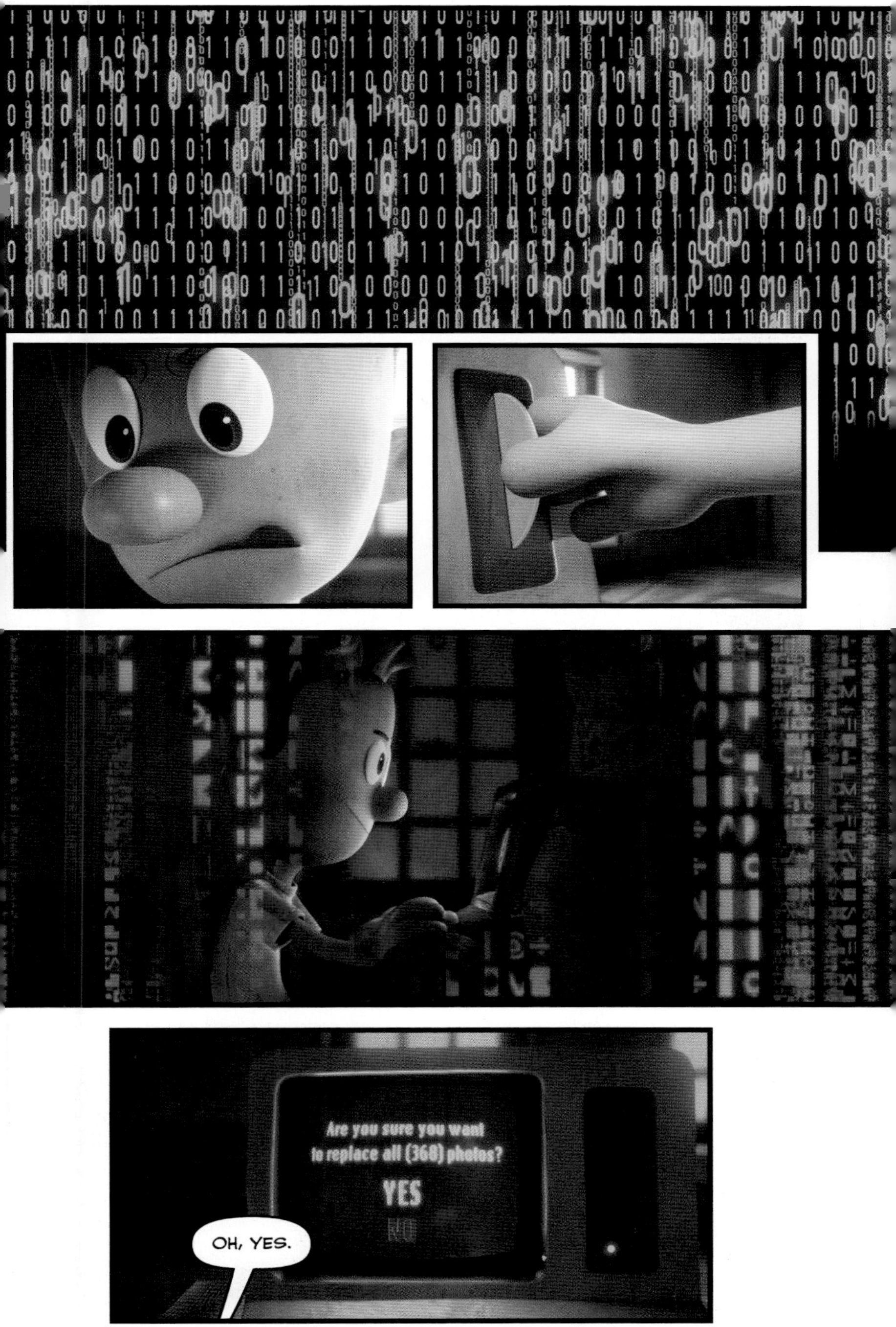
Are you sure you want
to replace all (368) photos?
YES
NO
OH, YES.

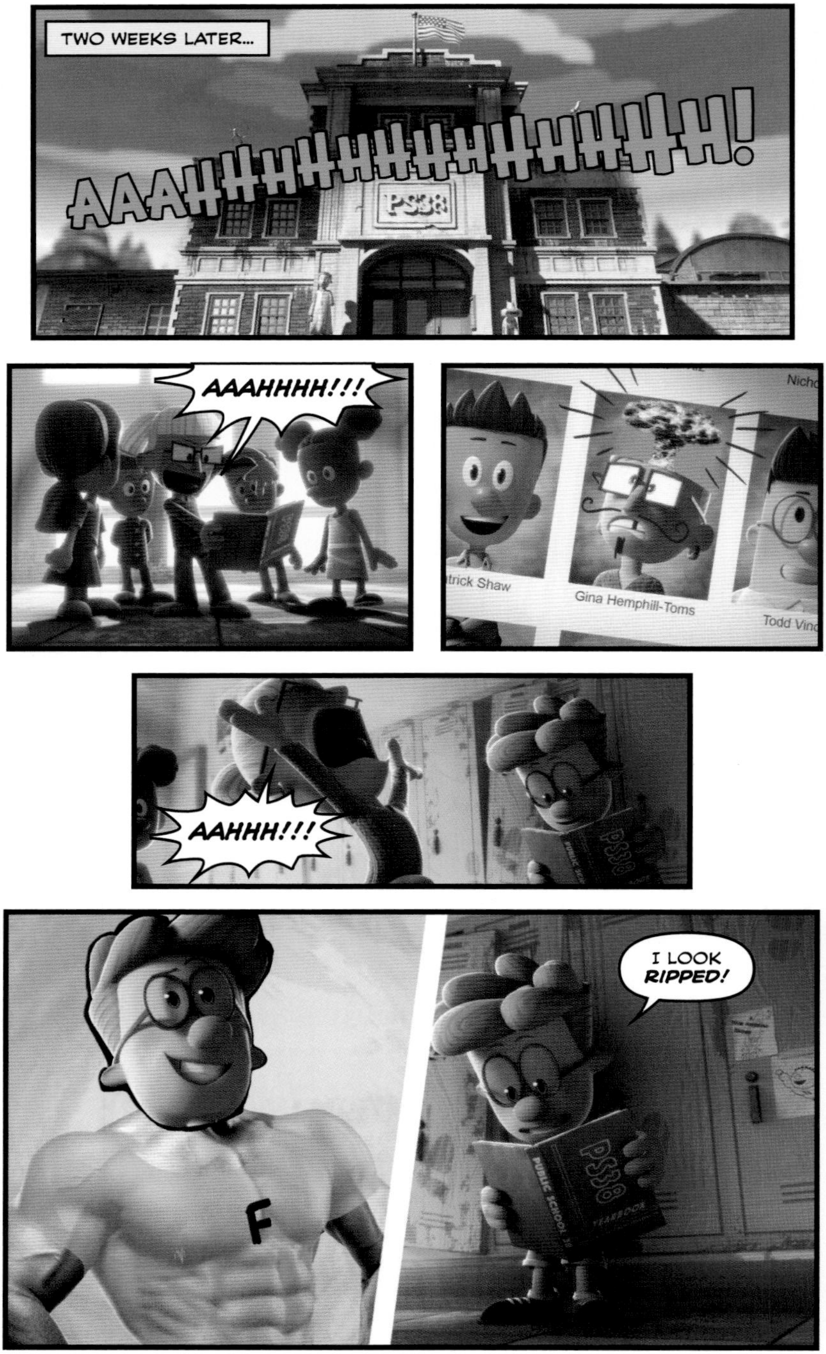
TWO WEEKS LATER...
AAAHHHHHHHHHHHHHH!
PS38
AAAHHHH!!!
trick Shaw
Gina Hemphill-Toms
Todd Vin
Nich
AAHHH!!!
PS38
I LOOK
RIPPED!
F
PS38
PUBLIC SCHOOL 38
YEARBOOK

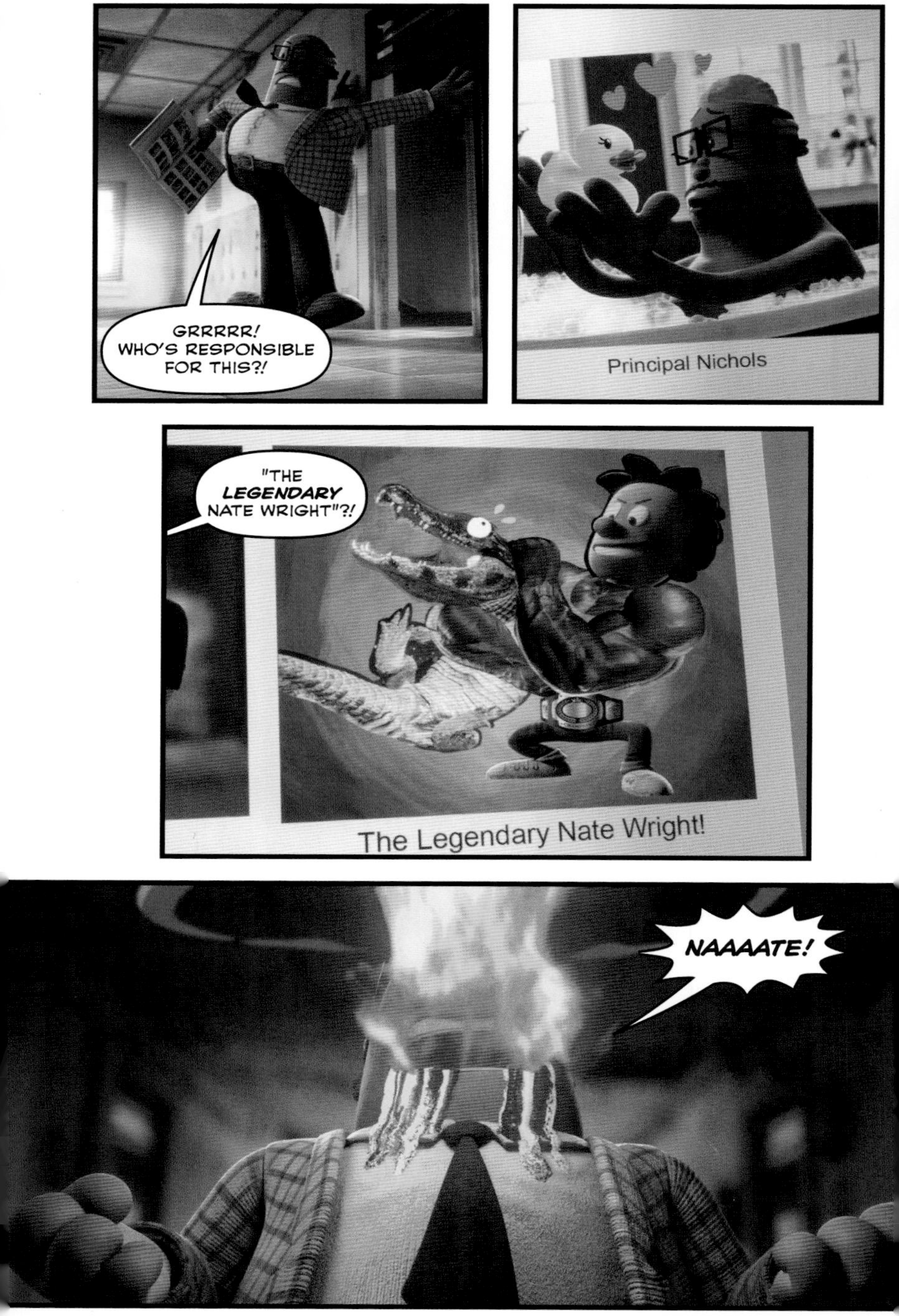
GRRRRR! WHO'S RESPONSIBLE FOR THIS?!
Principal Nichols
"THE *LEGENDARY* NATE WRIGHT"?!
The Legendary Nate Wright!
NAAAATE!

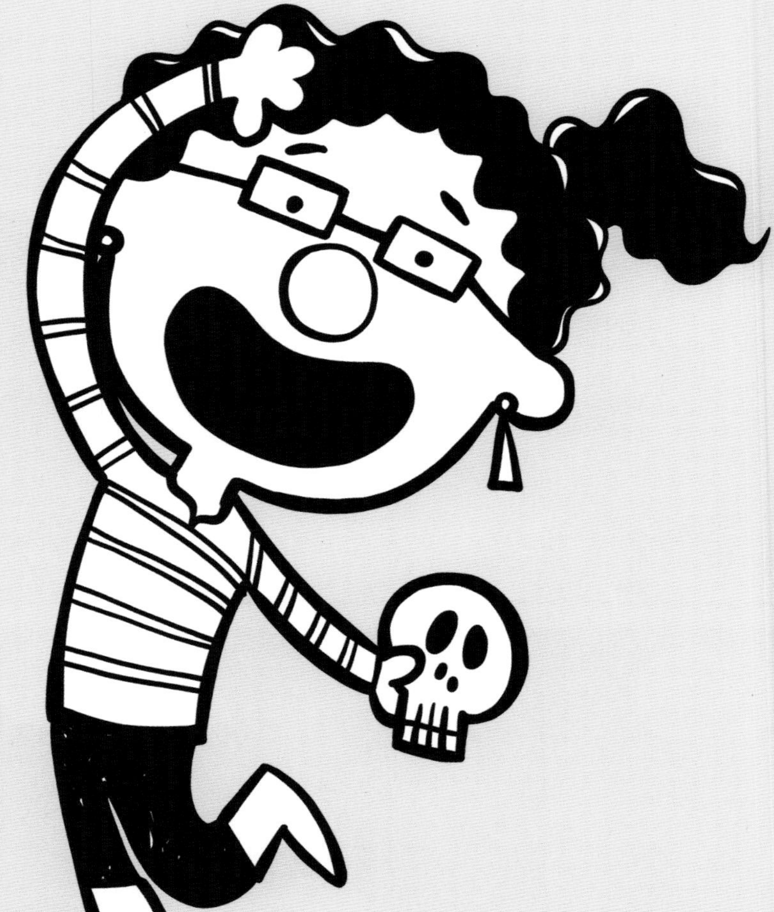

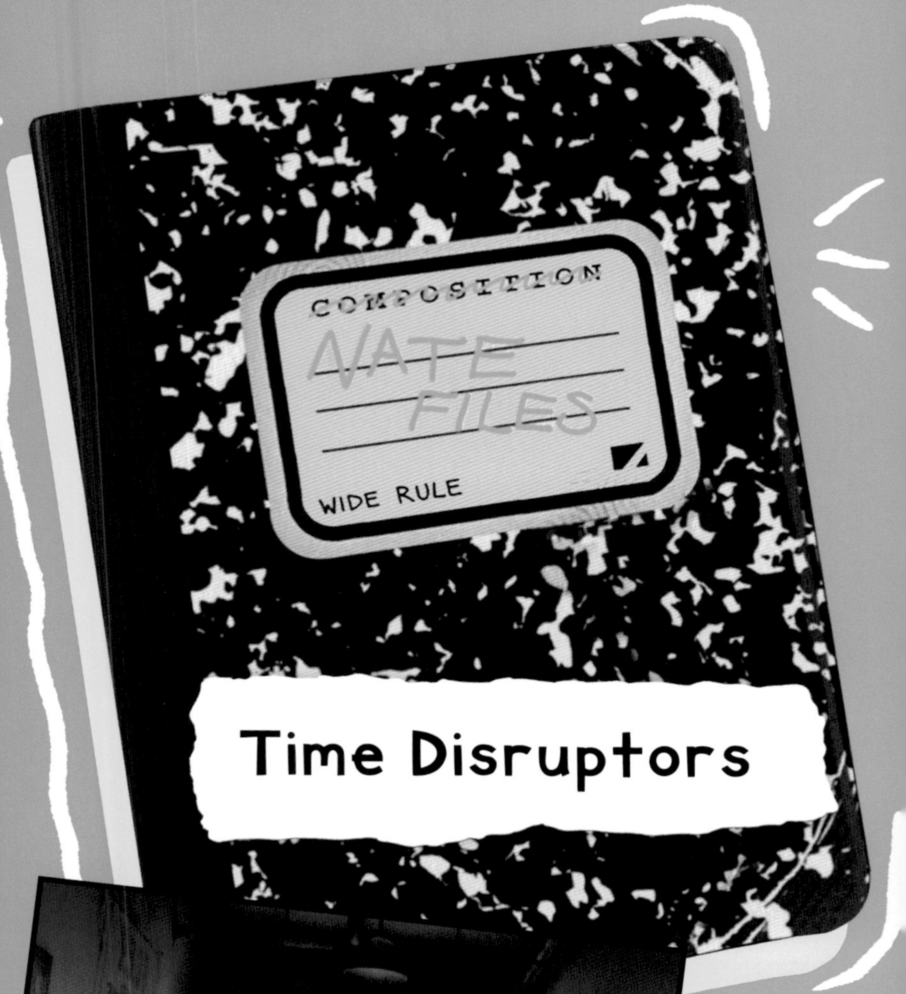
COMPOSITION
NATE FILES
WIDE RULE

Time Disruptors

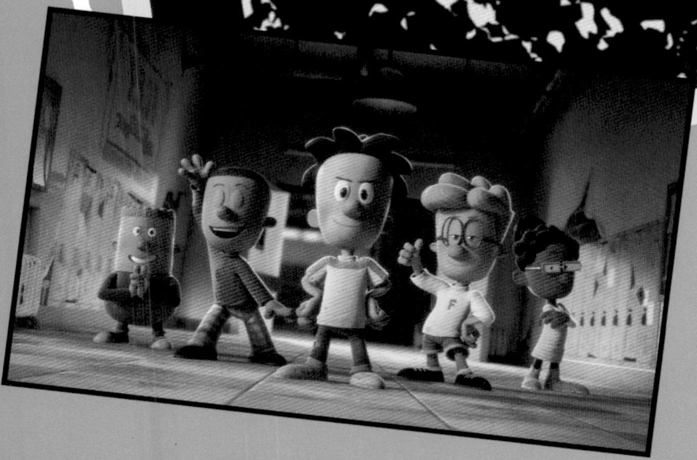

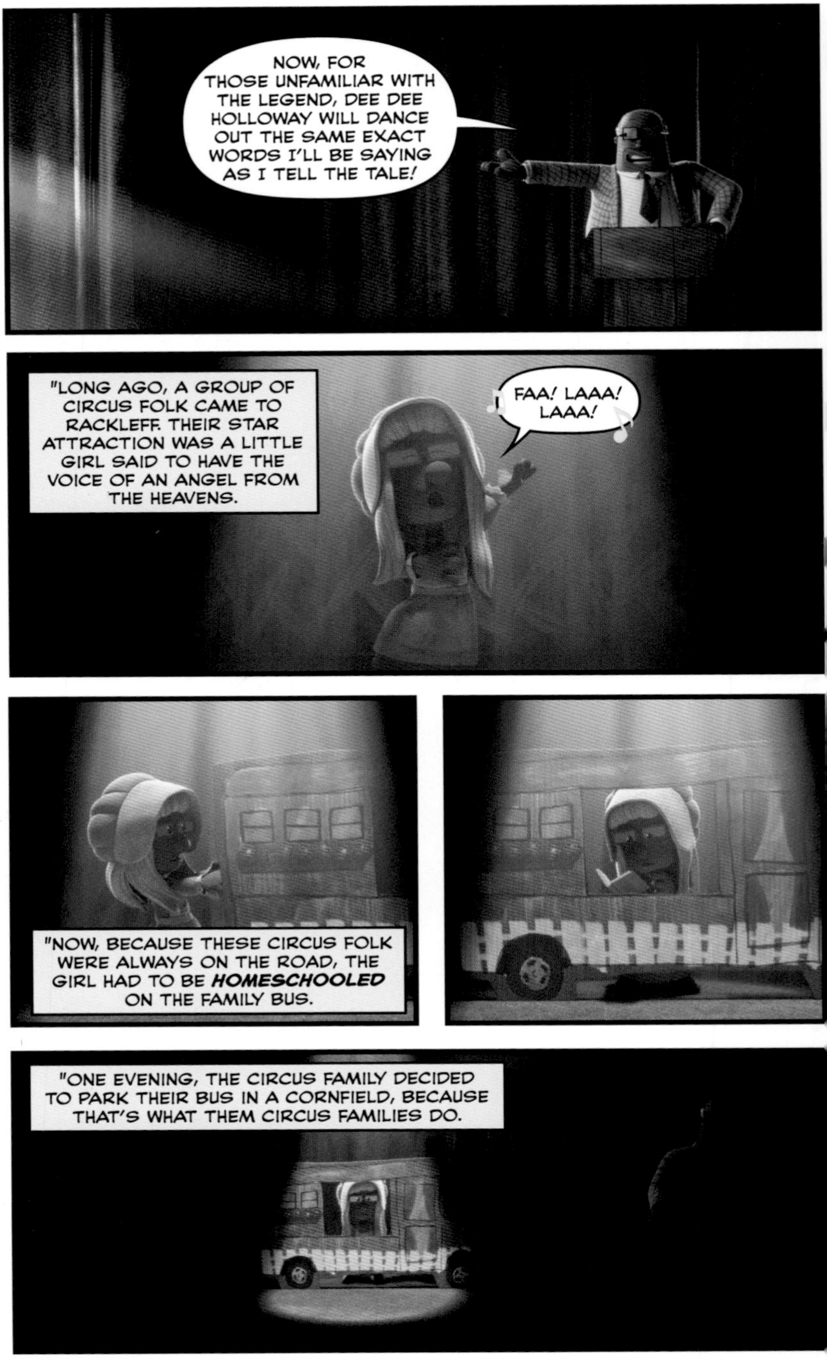
NOW, FOR THOSE UNFAMILIAR WITH THE LEGEND, DEE DEE HOLLOWAY WILL DANCE OUT THE SAME EXACT WORDS I'LL BE SAYING AS I TELL THE TALE!
"LONG AGO, A GROUP OF CIRCUS FOLK CAME TO RACKLEFF. THEIR STAR ATTRACTION WAS A LITTLE GIRL SAID TO HAVE THE VOICE OF AN ANGEL FROM THE HEAVENS.
FAA! LAAA! LAAA!
"NOW, BECAUSE THESE CIRCUS FOLK WERE ALWAYS ON THE ROAD, THE GIRL HAD TO BE ***HOMESCHOOLED*** ON THE FAMILY BUS.
"ONE EVENING, THE CIRCUS FAMILY DECIDED TO PARK THEIR BUS IN A CORNFIELD, BECAUSE THAT'S WHAT THEM CIRCUS FAMILIES DO.

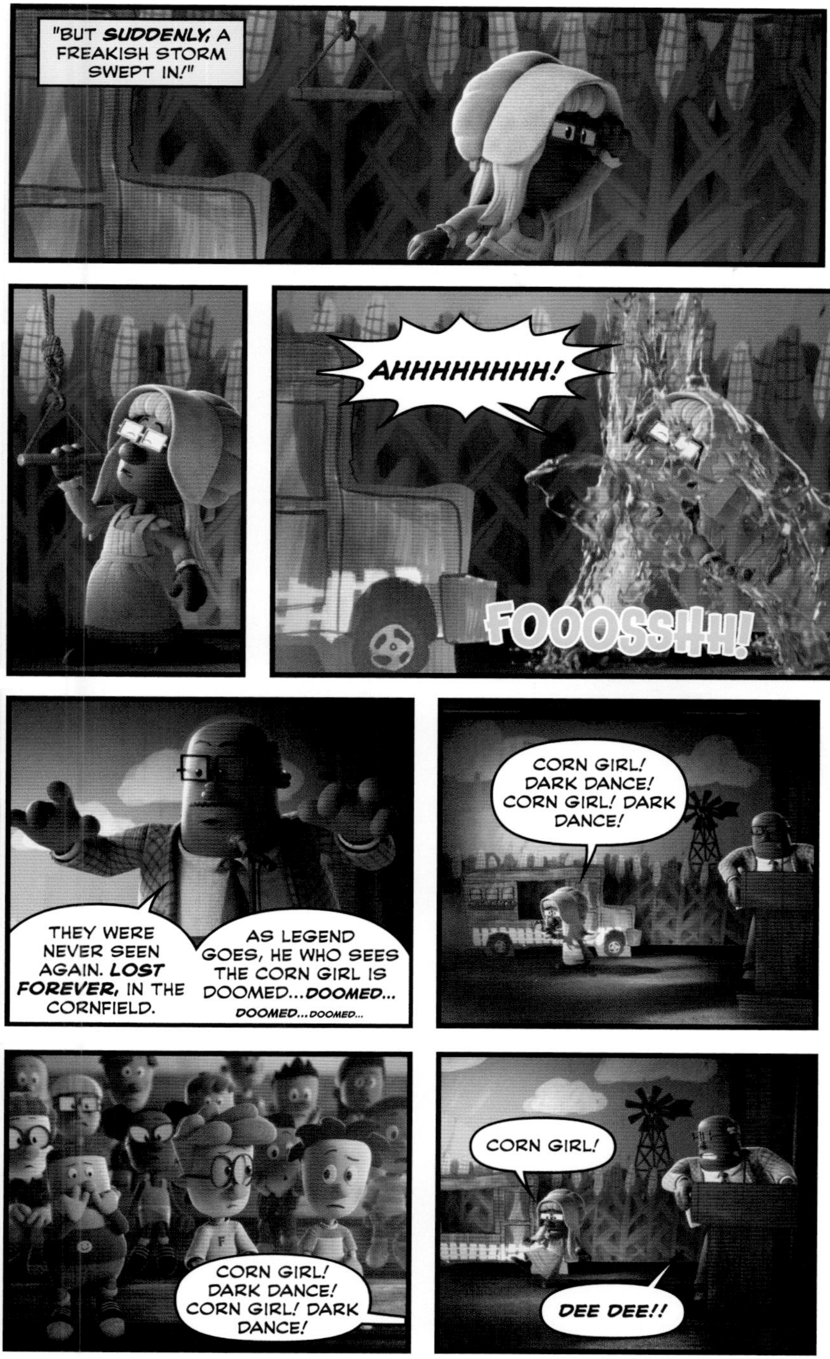
"BUT SUDDENLY, A FREAKISH STORM SWEPT IN!"
AHHHHHHHH!
FOOOSSHH!
THEY WERE NEVER SEEN AGAIN. LOST FOREVER, IN THE CORNFIELD.
AS LEGEND GOES, HE WHO SEES THE CORN GIRL IS DOOMED...DOOMED... DOOMED...DOOMED...
CORN GIRL! DARK DANCE! CORN GIRL! DARK DANCE!
CORN GIRL! DARK DANCE! CORN GIRL! DARK DANCE!
CORN GIRL!
DEE DEE!!

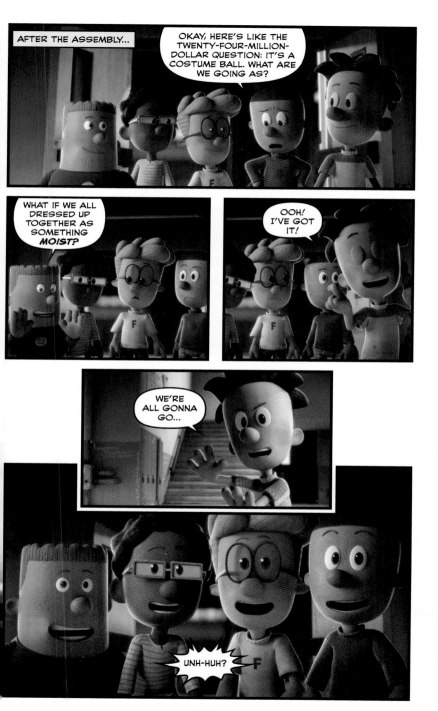

143

144

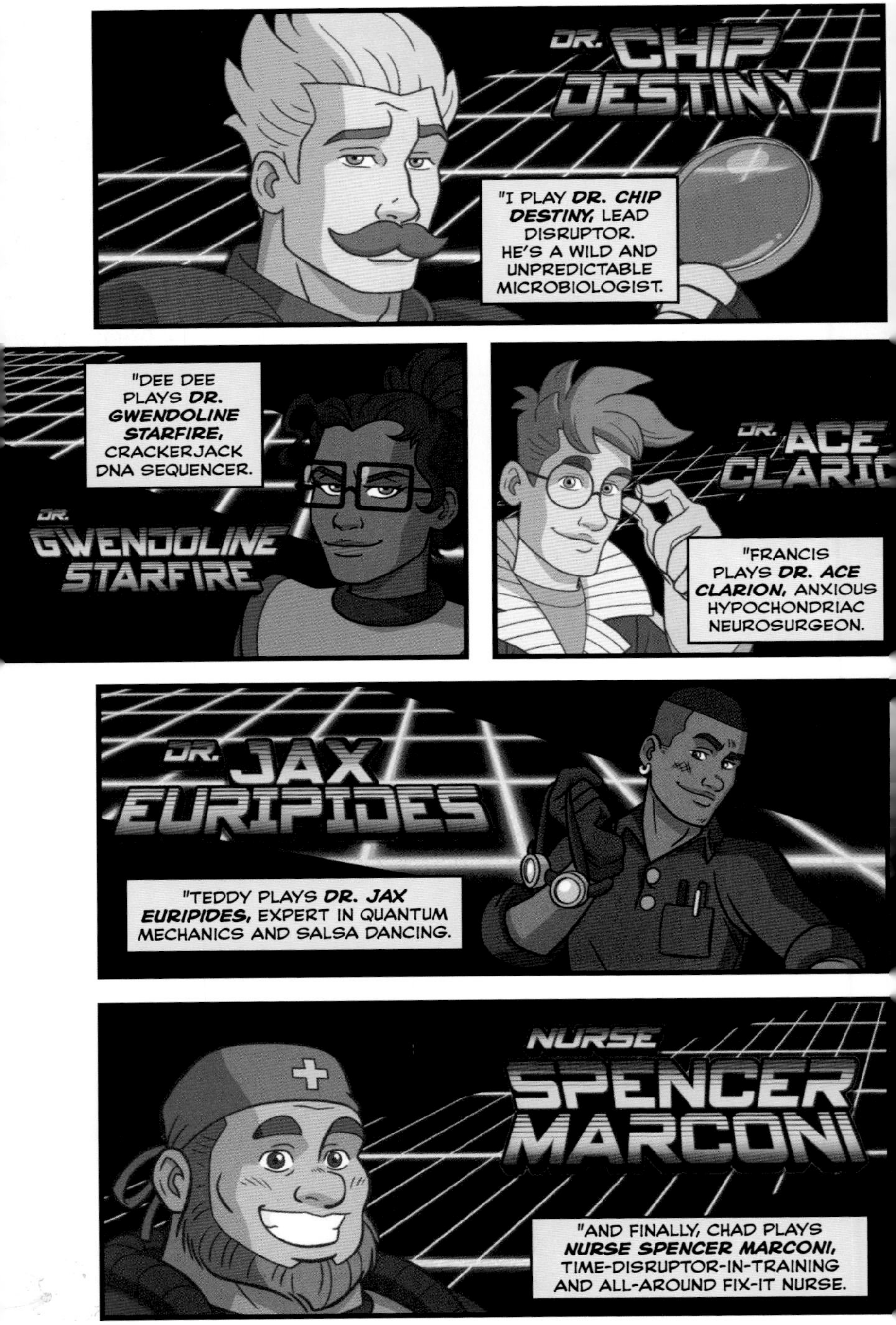
DR. CHIP DESTINY
"I PLAY DR. CHIP DESTINY, LEAD DISRUPTOR. HE'S A WILD AND UNPREDICTABLE MICROBIOLOGIST.
"DEE DEE PLAYS DR. GWENDOLINE STARFIRE, CRACKERJACK DNA SEQUENCER.
DR. GWENDOLINE STARFIRE
DR. ACE
"FRANCIS PLAYS DR. ACE CLARION, ANXIOUS HYPOCHONDRIAC NEUROSURGEON.
DR. JAX EURIPIDES
"TEDDY PLAYS DR. JAX EURIPIDES, EXPERT IN QUANTUM MECHANICS AND SALSA DANCING.
NURSE SPENCER MARCONI
"AND FINALLY, CHAD PLAYS NURSE SPENCER MARCONI, TIME-DISRUPTOR-IN-TRAINING AND ALL-AROUND FIX-IT NURSE.

AFTER SCHOOL.
I'M FAST
HMMM?
VWOOSH!
GRRRRR!

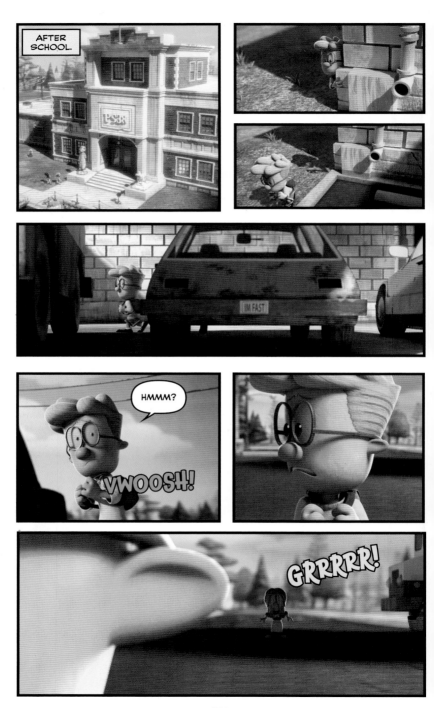

PFF! PFF! PFF!

≋GASP!≋

CORN GIRL....

WHOOAA!

Evil!

JEFFERSON MIDDLE SCHOOL

Corporate Funded

PPPPBTT!

HELLO?

AHHHHHH!

CRASH!

NICE JUMP!
GOTTA WORK ON THAT LANDING, THOUGH.
WAIT FOR ME!
HEHEHEHEHE!

157

I, UH...
WAS THAT
TODAY?
FOURTEEN
HOURS, SEVEN
MINUTES, AND SIX
SECONDS BEFORE
OUR VERY FIRST
P.S. 38 DANCE...
...I MEAN
WOW.
WOOOOW!
I GOTTA
SPLIT!
WHAT?!

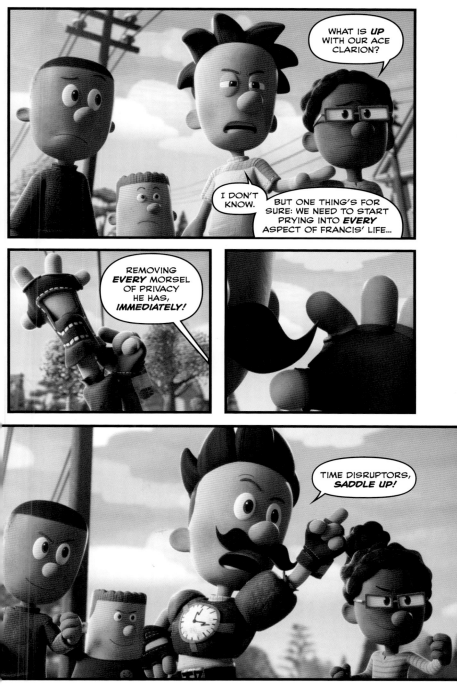

HMMMM...

WOOF?

SNIF! SNIF!

AHHHHH!!!

TIME DISRUPTORS, IT IS GOIN' DOWN.

SNAP!

OOF!

WHAM!

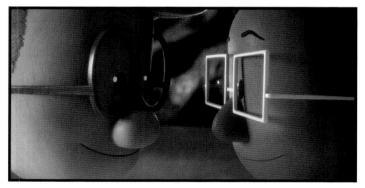

WHAT THE?!

WHAM!

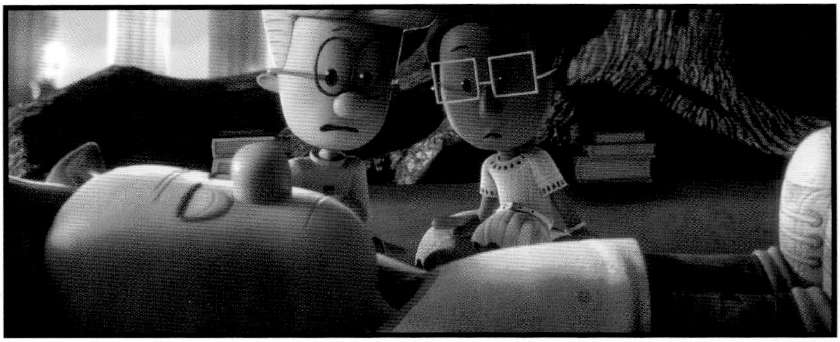

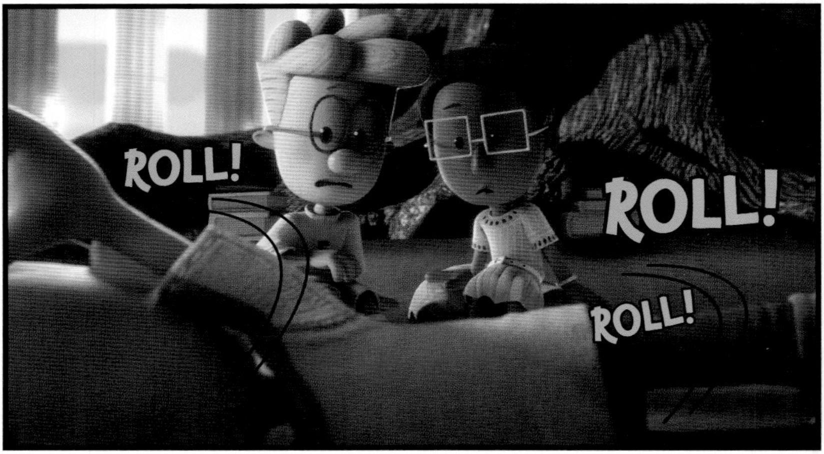
ROLL!
ROLL!
ROLL!

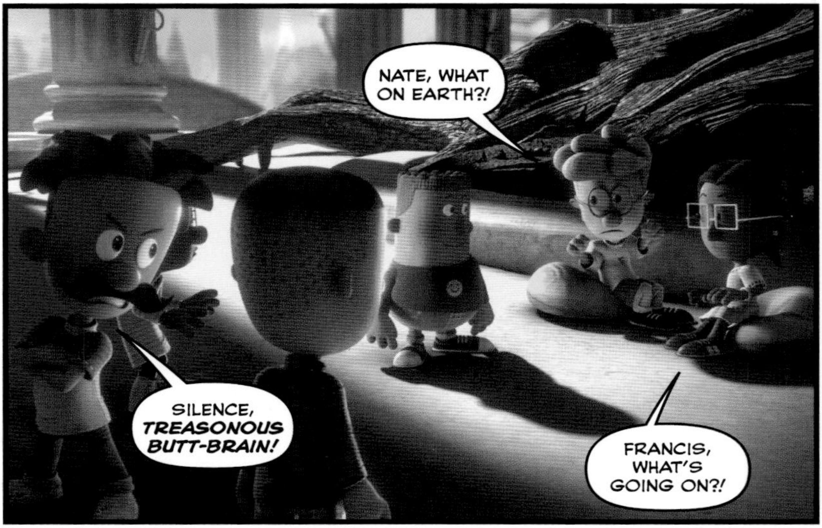
NATE, WHAT ON EARTH?!
SILENCE, *TREASONOUS BUTT-BRAIN!*
FRANCIS, WHAT'S GOING ON?!

WAIT A MINUTE...IT'S JUST LIKE THE PLOT OF THE TIME DISRUPTORS' CLASSIC, *"CRISIS ON PLANET BRAIN"!*

SABINA, I'M SORRY, ABOUT... ALL OF THIS.

NO, *I'M* SORRY. I DIDN'T THINK YOU TUTORING ME WAS SUCH A BIG DEAL.

IT'S NOT. CAN I CALL YOU LATER?

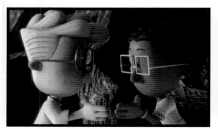

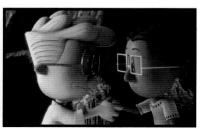

172

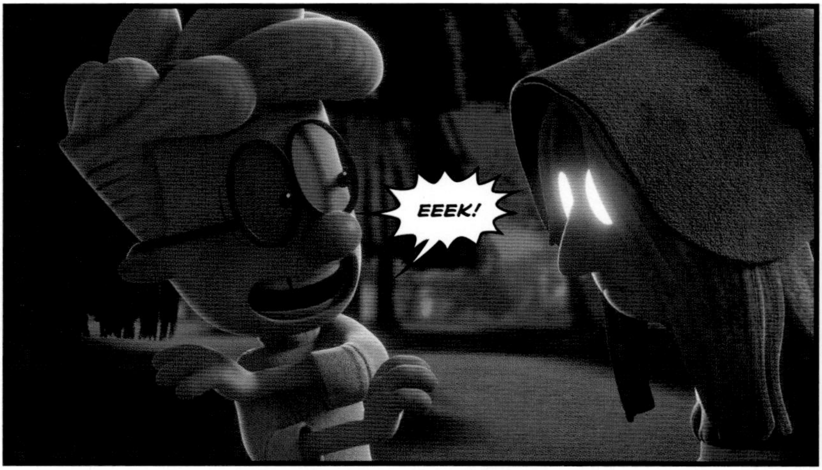
EEEK!

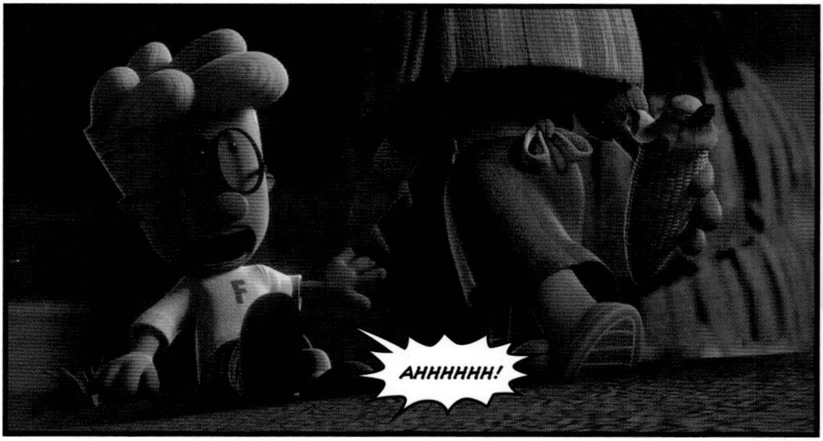
AHHHHHH!

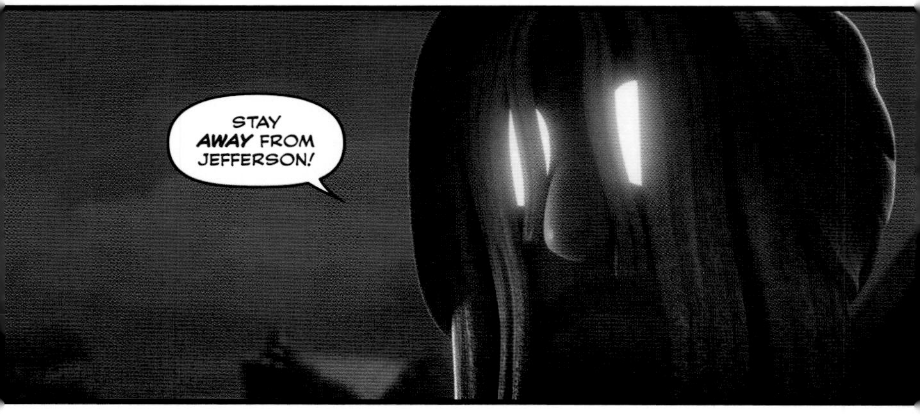
STAY AWAY FROM JEFFERSON!

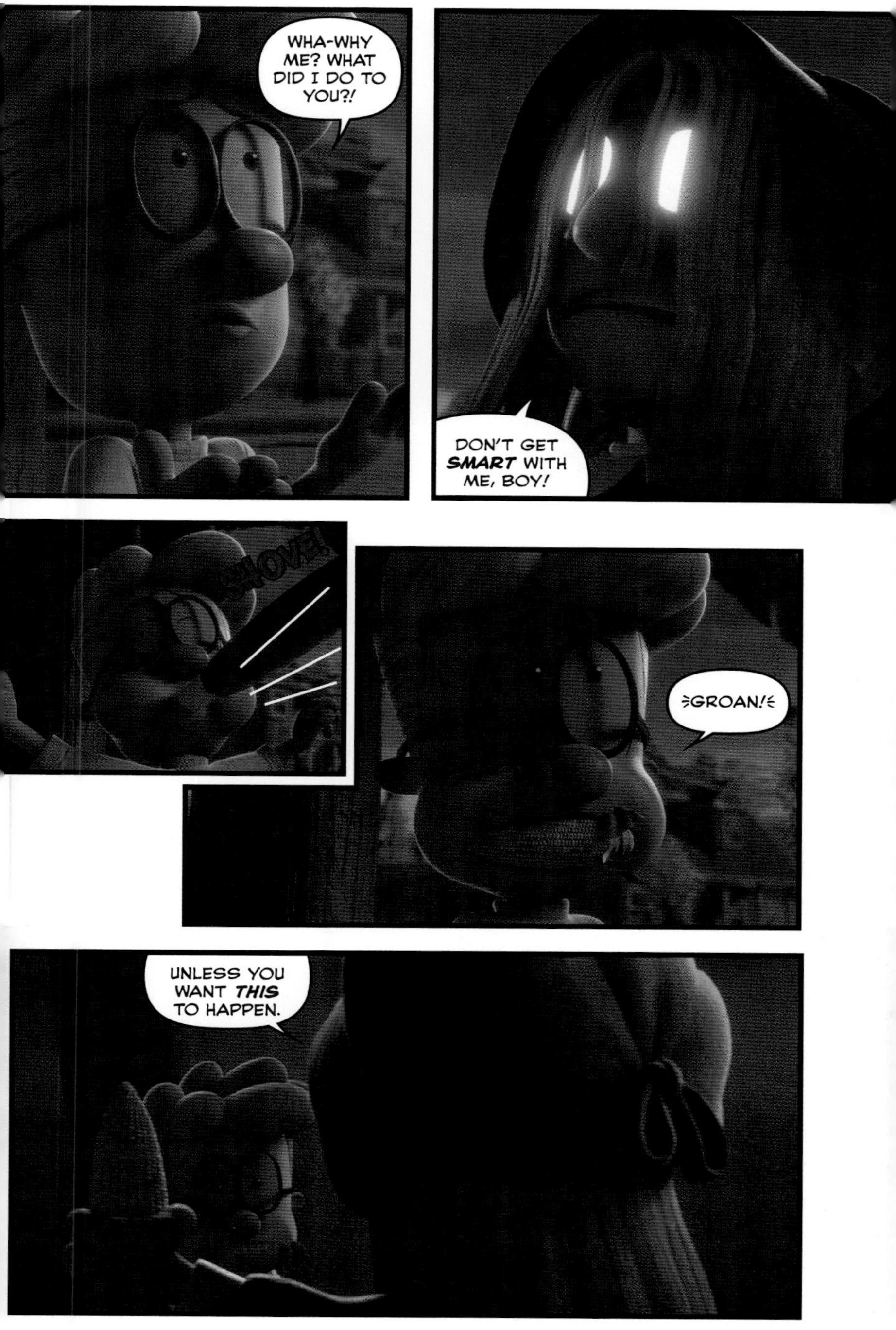
WHA-WHY ME? WHAT DID I DO TO YOU?!
DON'T GET SMART WITH ME, BOY!
SHOVE!
GROAN!
UNLESS YOU WANT THIS TO HAPPEN.

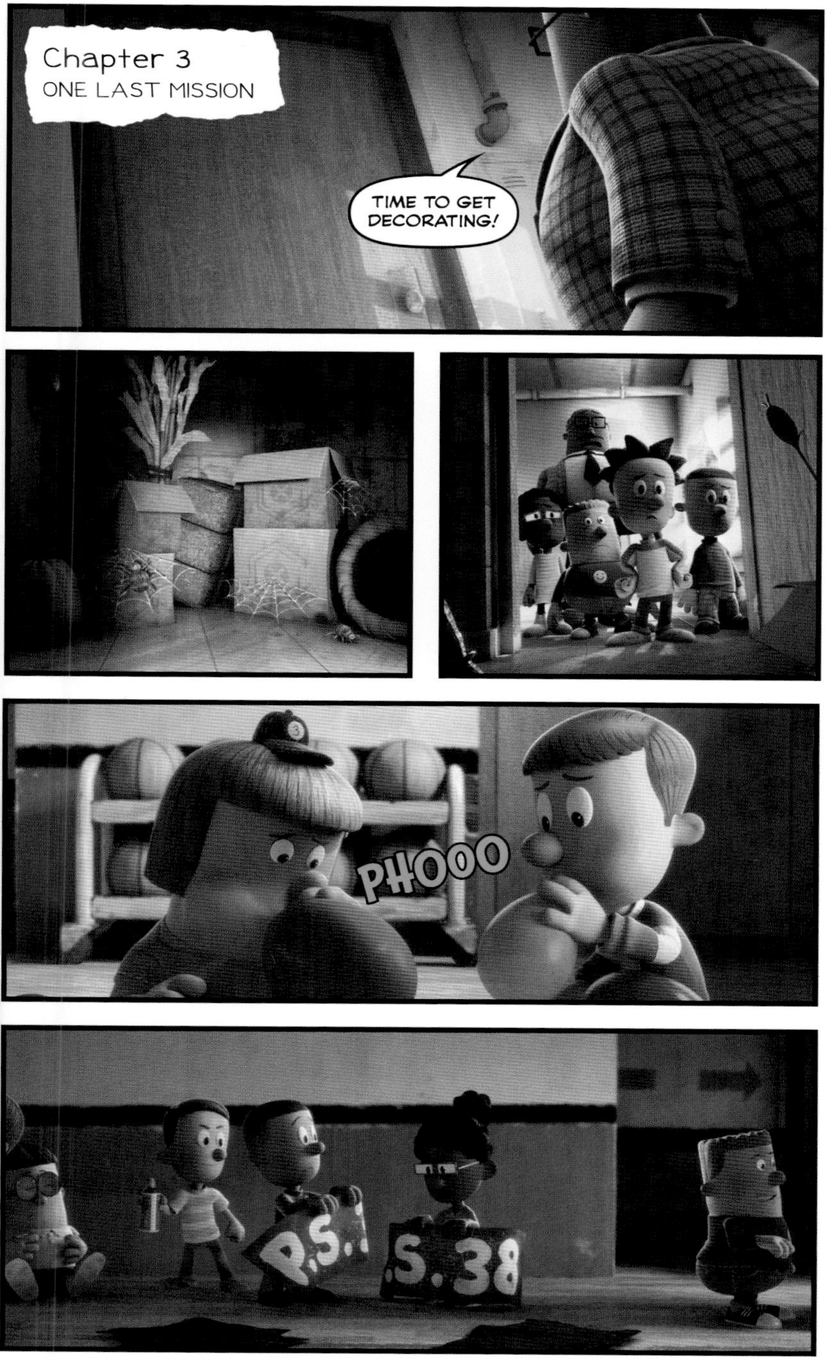
Chapter 3
ONE LAST MISSION
TIME TO GET DECORATING!
PHOOO

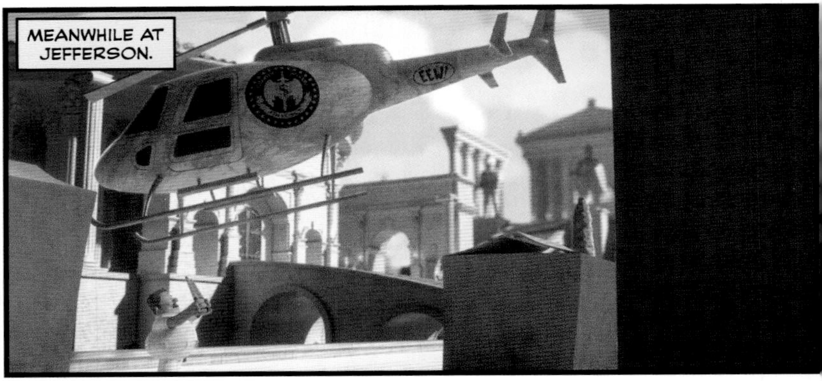
MEANWHILE AT JEFFERSON.
EEW!

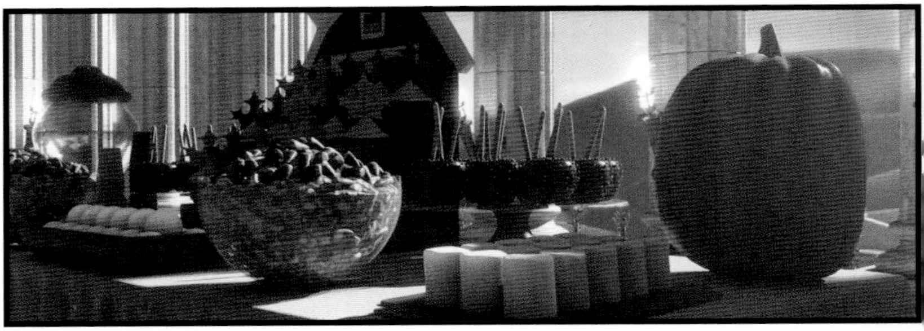

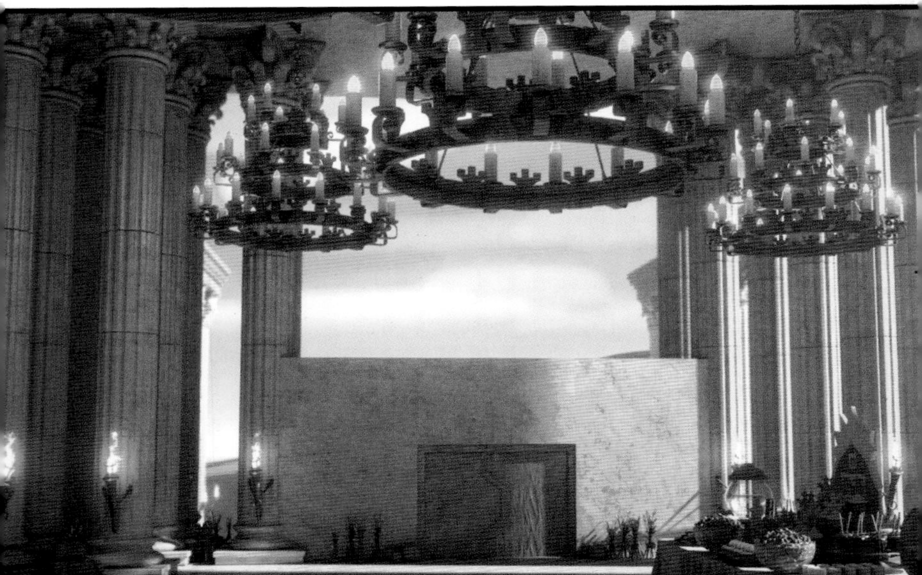

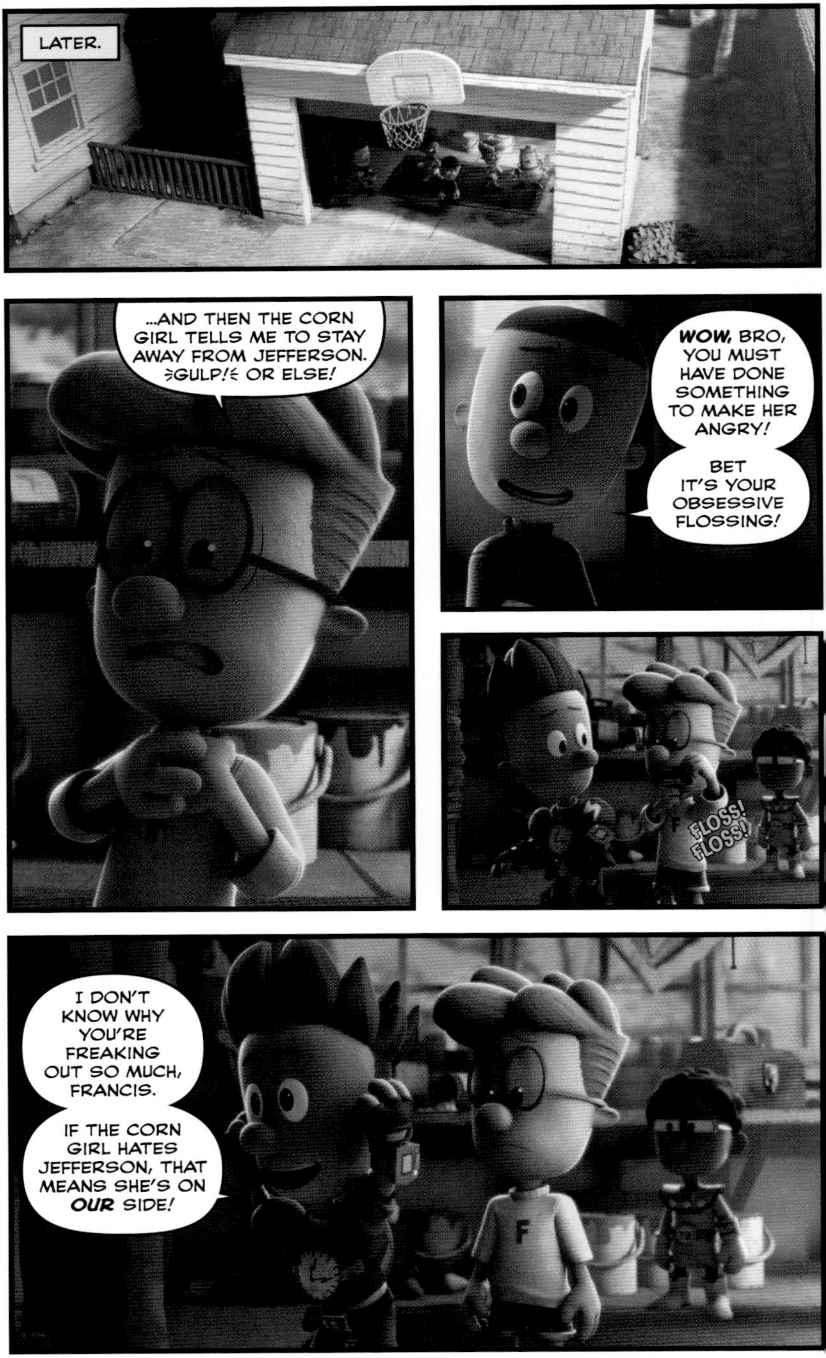
LATER.
...AND THEN THE CORN GIRL TELLS ME TO STAY AWAY FROM JEFFERSON. ⋛GULP!⋚ OR ELSE!
WOW, BRO, YOU MUST HAVE DONE SOMETHING TO MAKE HER ANGRY!
BET IT'S YOUR OBSESSIVE FLOSSING!
FLOSS! FLOSS!
I DON'T KNOW WHY YOU'RE FREAKING OUT SO MUCH, FRANCIS.
IF THE CORN GIRL HATES JEFFERSON, THAT MEANS SHE'S ON OUR SIDE!

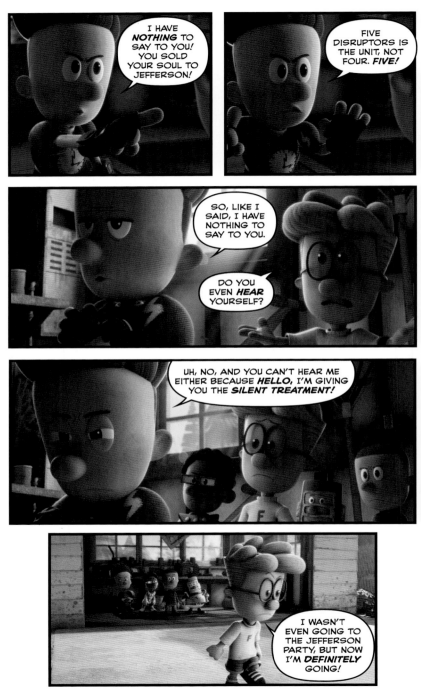

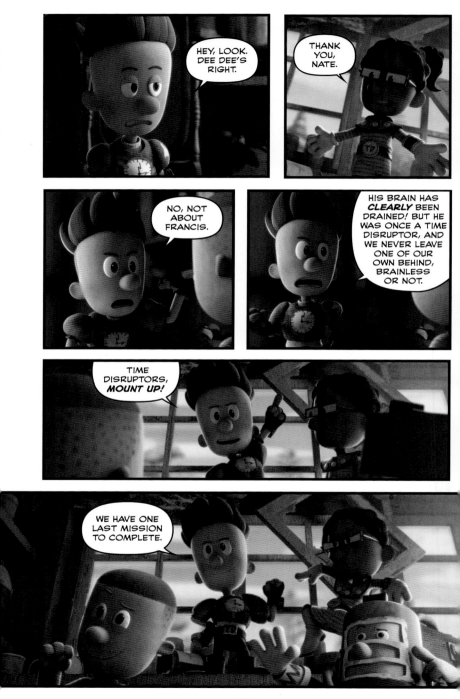

Chapter 4
TAKING CONTROL
OF OUR DESTINY

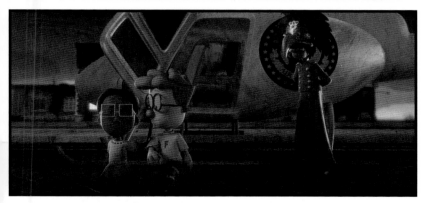

I FEEL OUT OF PLACE IN THESE CLOTHES!

STOP OVERTHINKING IT. NOBODY'S GONNA NOTICE.

YOU HAVE *PRECISELY* TWO SECONDS TO EXPLAIN WHATEVER IT IS YOU THINK YOU'RE WEARING!

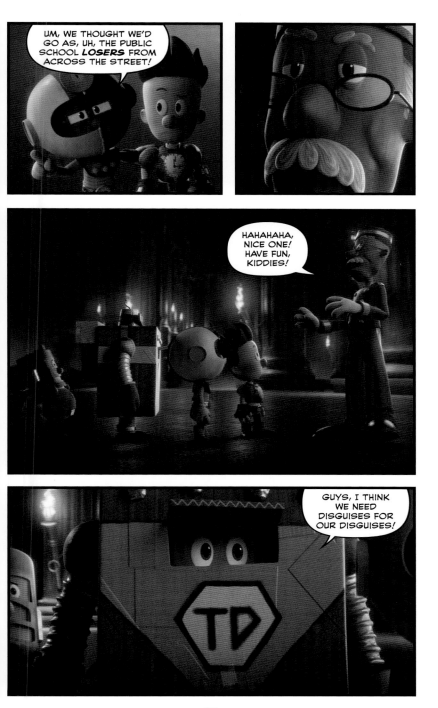

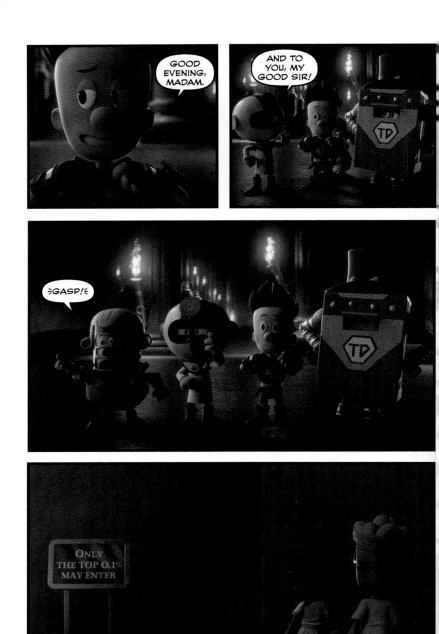

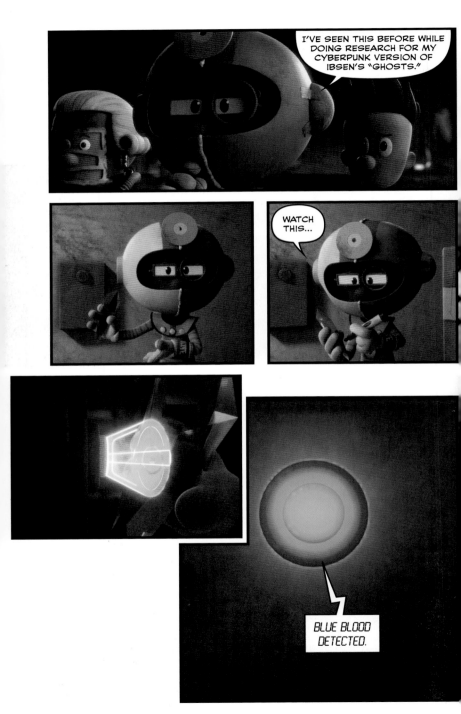

CREAK!

CHAD!

SHOO! SHOO!

IF THIS WERE A TIME DISRUPTOR MOVIE, MESSING WITH FRANCIS FINDING HAPPINESS WOULD RESULT IN SOME FUTURE FILLED WITH UNTOLD HORRORS.

AHHH!
SKID!
AHHHH!
WHAM!
OOMPH!

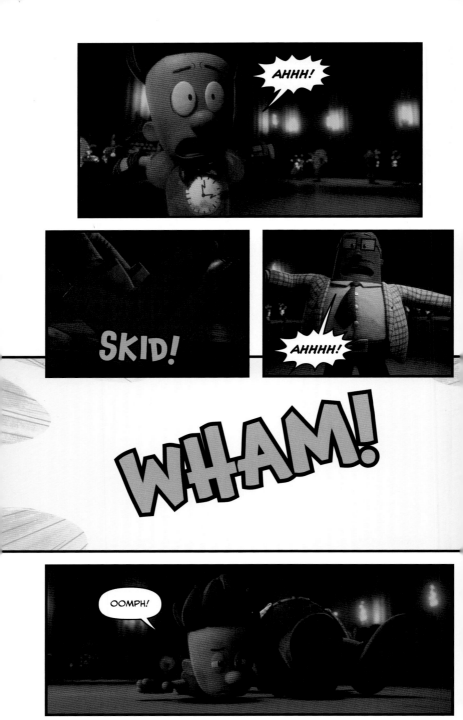

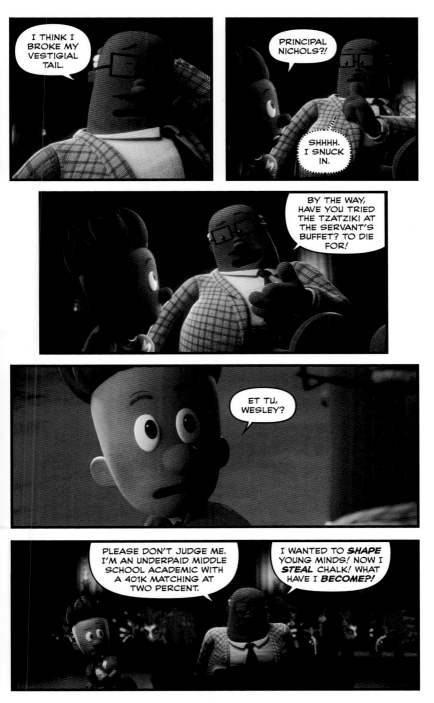

205

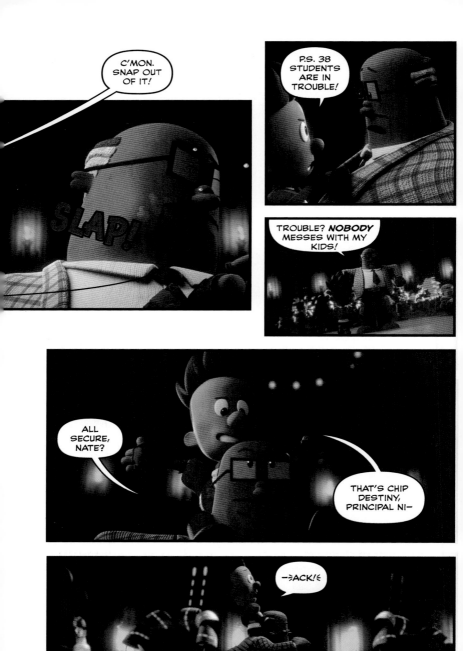

GULP!
GOT YA, CHAD
WHAM!
HUH?!
AAAAHH!!
YOU'RE MINE NOW!
LET'S GO!

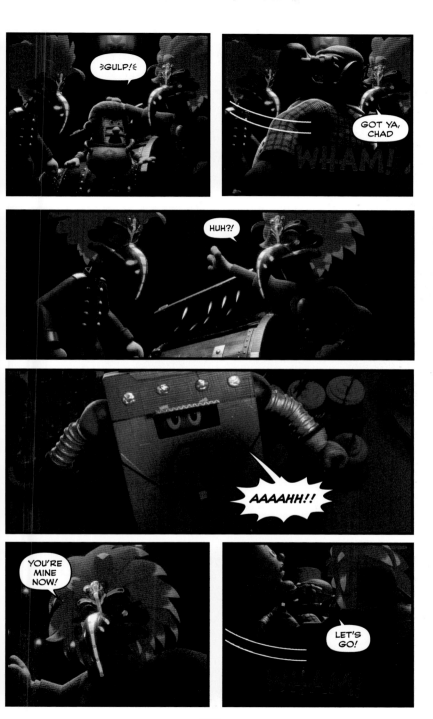

NATE!

YOU **CRASHED** THE JEFFERSON MASQUERADE BALL?

NO, N-N-NO, IT'S NOT WHAT YOU THINK.

213

214

BWA-HA-HA! I WARNED YOU, STAY AWAY FROM JEFFERSON!
NOW EVERYONE'S GOING TO GET CORNED!
RUN!
AHHHHHHH!

216

FRIENDS?
FRIENDS.

AAAHHHHH!

AHHHHH!

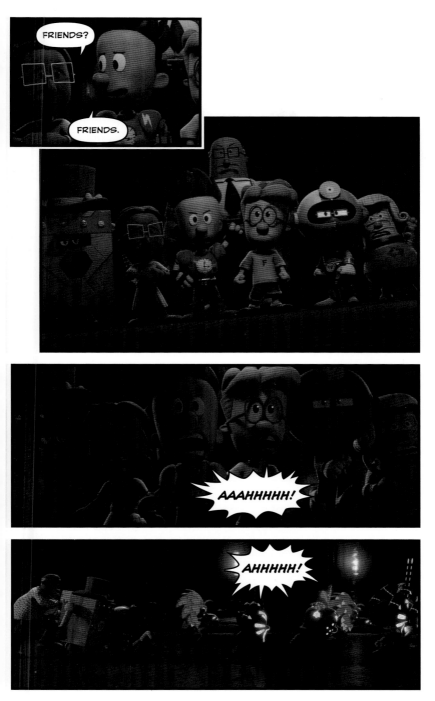

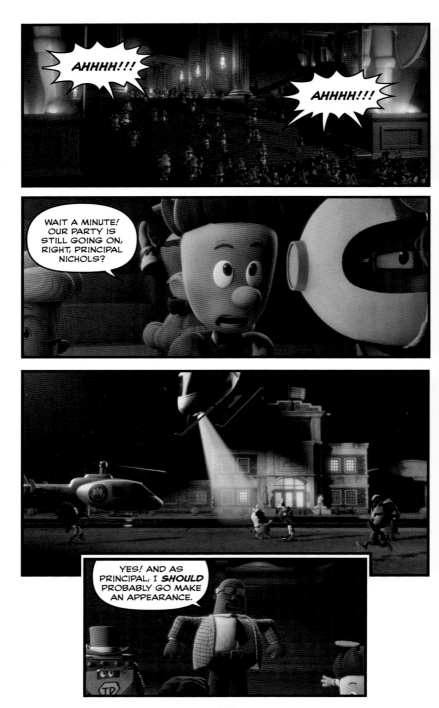

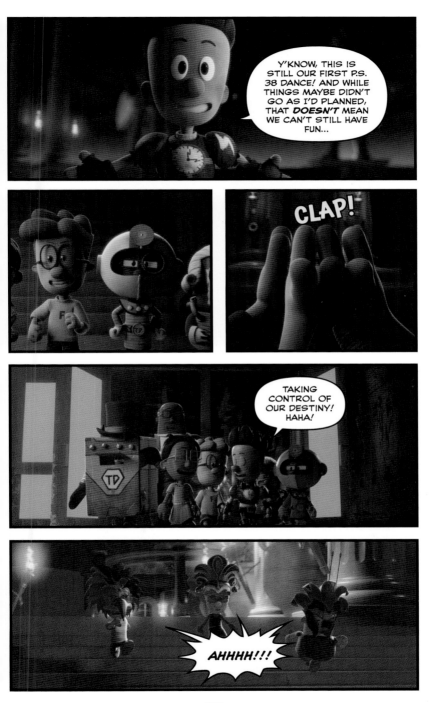

SHOW CREDITS

WRITTEN BY
MITCH WATSON
ELLIOTT OWEN
SARAH ALLAN
ERIC SHAW

STORYBOARD ARTISTS
KAT CHAN
LAKE FAMA
HEATHER GREGERSEN
KIMBERLY JO MILLS
JIM MORTENSEN
JEFF DEGRANDIS
BRADLEY GOODCHILD
ZOË MOSS
KYLE NESWALD
KEVIN SINGLETON
GREY WHITE
SEBASTIAN DUCLOS
RAY GEIGER
BRANDON WARREN
MARIANA YOVANOVICH
MARIA NGUYEN
MEG SYVERUD
COLIN HECK
MIKE DOUGHERTY
VICTORIA HARRIS
BENJAMIN HOLM
TANNER JOHNSON

CONSULTING PRODUCER
LINCOLN PEIRCE

CO-PRODUCER
BRIDGET MCMEEL

ART DIRECTOR
DAVID SKELLY

CG SUPERVISOR
CHRISTINA LAFERLA

SUPERVISING PRODUCER
JIM MORTENSEN

PRODUCER
AMY MCKENNA

EXECUTIVE PRODUCER
JOHN COHEN

EXECUTIVE PRODUCER
MITCH WATSON
HEAD WRITER
EMILY BRUNDIGE
STAFF WRITERS
SARAH ALLAN
BEN LAPIDES

ASSOCIATE PRODUCER
TAYLOR BRADBURY
STORYBOARD REVISIONISTS
ANDREW CAPUANO
MISTY MARSDEN
JAZZLYN WEAVER

SCRIPT COORDINATOR
LISSY KLATCHKO
PRODUCTION COORDINATORS
BRANDON CHAU
CLAIRE NORRIS
CARLINA WILLIAMS
LOGAN YUZNA
SIENNA SERTL
ASSET PRODUCTION COORDINATORS
DIANA GRIGORIAN
SEAN MCPARTLAND

PRODUCTION ASSISTANTS
CYNTHIA CORTEZ
SARA FISHER
DARREN OJEDA
NATASHA SHIELDS
HANNAH JANE GOULDEN
CAITLYN KURILICH
AJ SHENEFELT
EXECUTIVE ASSISTANT
ALEX VAN DER HOEK

CHARACTER DESIGNERS
ROBERT BROWN
JUN LEE
JOCELYN SEPULVEDA
BACKGROUND DESIGNERS
PETER J. DELUCA
GRACE KUM
BECCA RAMOS
JOSH WESSLING
PROP DESIGNERS
ZACHARY CLARKSON
TYLER WILLIAM GENTRY
RC MONTESQUIEU
SHANNON PRESTON
2D DESIGNER
VICKI SCOTT
BACKGROUND PAINTERS
NATALIE FRANSCIONI-KARP
JONATHAN HOEKSTRA
QUINTIN PUEBLA
PATRICK MORGAN

LEAD CG GENERALIST
VYPAC VOUER
LEAD CHARACTER TECHNICAL DIRECTOR
AREEBA RAZA KHAN
LEAD LOOK DEVELOPMENT ARTIST
CANDICE STEPHENSON
LOOK DEVELOPMENT ARTIST
JUAN GIL

COLOR CORRECTION SERVICES
ROUNDABOUT ENTERTAINMENT
COLORIST
BRYAN MCMAHAN

CG GENERALIST
THOMAS THOMAS III

ANIMATION DIRECTOR
DENNIS SHELBY
MARK LEE
**LIGHTING & COMPOSITING
DIRECTOR**
DARREN D. KINER
CODY BURKE
ASSOCIATE ART DIRECTOR
SAM KOJI HALE

2D ANIMATION SERVICES
XENTRIX TOONS
FOR XENTRIX TOONS
CREATIVE DIRECTOR
HARRIS CABEROY
PRODUCTION MANAGER
SHERYLEN CAOILI
FX SUPERVISOR
KERWIN OJO
PRODUCTION TEAM
ARA KATRIN LUDOVICO
JANILLE BIANCA TUDELA

SPECIAL THANKS
BRIAN ROBBINS
RAMSEY NAITO
BRIAN KEANE
ANGELIQUE YEN
DANA CLUVERIUS
CLAUDIA SPINELLI

ANIMATION DEVELOPMENT
NATHAN SCHRAM
LESLIE WISHNEVSKI

CURRENT SERIES MANAGEMENT
NEIL WADE

**VICE PRESIDENT OF ANIMATION
PRODUCTION**
DEAN HOFF

**EXECUTIVE IN CHARGE FOR
NICKELODEON**
NATHAN SCHRAM

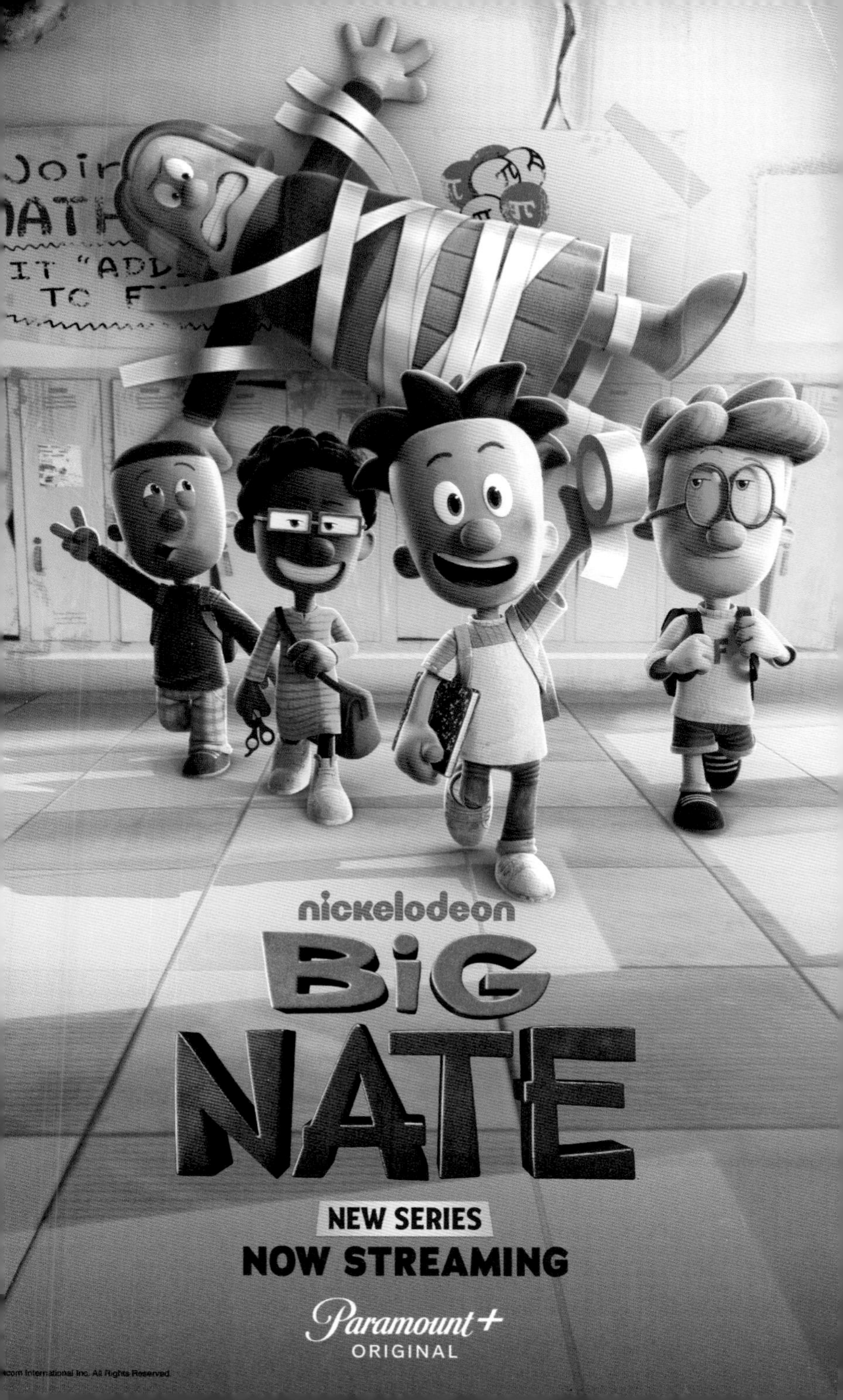
nickelodeon
BIG NATE
NEW SERIES
NOW STREAMING
Paramount+
ORIGINAL
International Inc. All Rights Reserved.

Complete Your *Big Nate* Collection

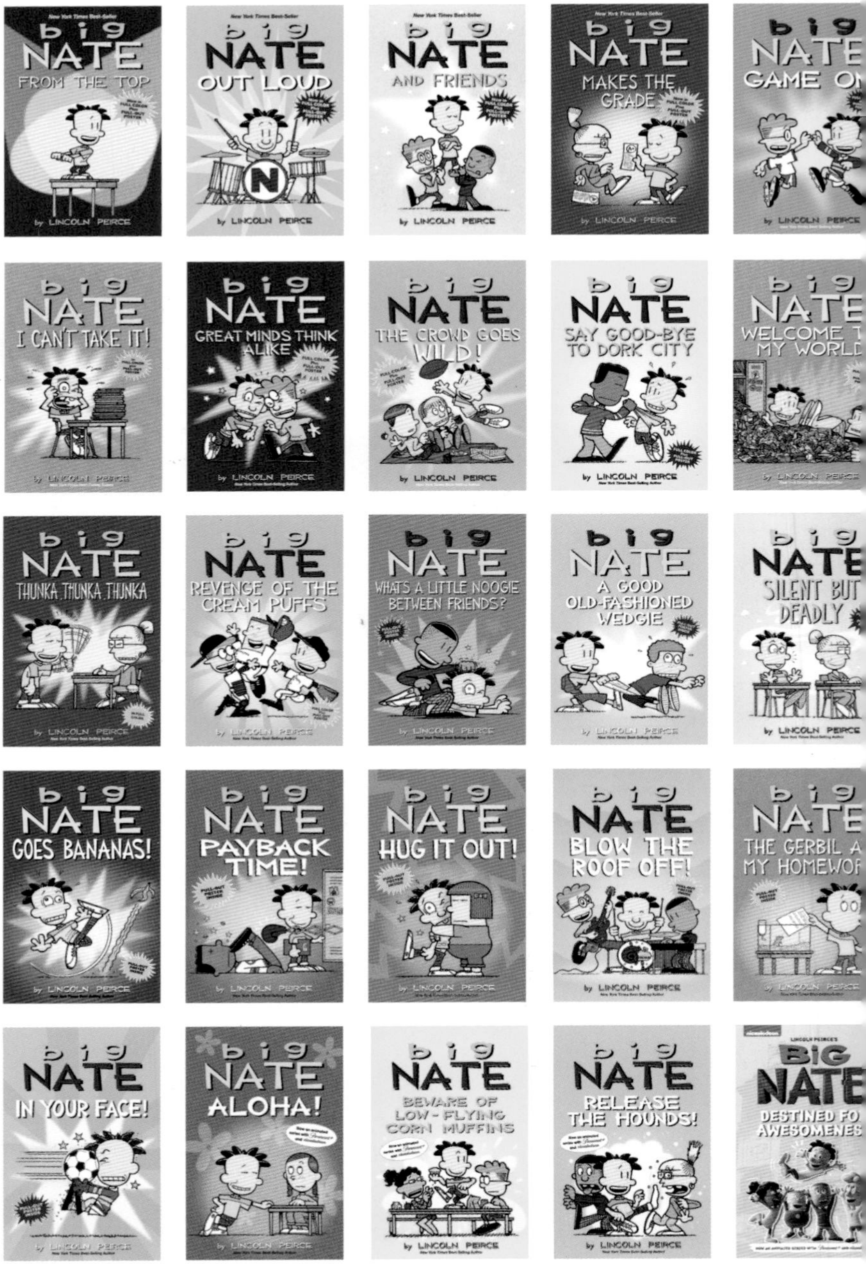
big NATE FROM THE TOP
big NATE OUT LOUD
big NATE AND FRIENDS
big NATE MAKES THE GRADE
big NATE GAME
big NATE I CAN'T TAKE IT!
big NATE GREAT MINDS THINK ALIKE
big NATE THE CROWD GOES WILD!
big NATE SAY GOOD-BYE TO DORK CITY
big WELCOME MY
big NATE THUNKA THUNKA THUNKA
big NATE REVENGE OF THE CREAM PUFFS
big NATE WHAT'S A LITTLE NOOGIE BETWEEN FRIENDS?
big NATE A GOOD OLD-FASHIONED WEDGIE
big SILENT DEADLY
big NATE GOES BANANAS!
big NATE PAYBACK TIME!
big NATE HUG IT OUT!
big NATE BLOW THE ROOF OFF!
big THE GERBIL MY
big NATE IN YOUR FACE!
big NATE ALOHA!
big NATE BEWARE OF LOW-FLYING CORN MUFFINS
big NATE RELEASE THE HOUNDS!
LINCOLN PEIRCE'S BIG
by LINCOLN PEIRCE